BLUE SAPPHIRE TEMPTATION

HIGH CLASS SOCIETY SERIES #1

SHERELLE GREEN

"Falling For Autumn isn't your typical romance. The main characters have flaws, baggage from their childhoods and past relationships, and vulnerabilities which made them seem realistic and relatable. Green does an excellent job in setting up the storyline, in using the secondary characters, and there's just enough sensuality and heat which balances out the love and romance. Falling For Autumn has set the bar high for the rest of the books in the romance genre."

— READING IN BLACK AND WHITE, TIFFANY TYLER

"Readers will definitely feel the heat as Green flirts with the line between erotica and romance. This story will make even the most skeptical person believe in fate and the idea of the universe working to bring two people together."

— RT BOOK REVIEWS

"Sherelle Green was absolutely consistent with this series. The writing was excellent, the story telling was great and the passion was FIRE!!!"

— BRAB BOOKCLUB, ALICIA AARON

To my very own romance hero. You stole my heart in 2005 and it's been yours ever since.

BLUE SAPPHIRE TEMPTATION

Logan "Lo" Sapphire has never backed down from a challenge, so she's convinced that she can persuade the stern and unyielding self-made millionaire to keep High Class Society a secret after he bursts into her office demanding to know his sister's whereabouts. The last thing Lo wants to do is go on a wild goose chase with a walking sex ad to find his sister, but maybe, just maybe, finding her will coax him into signing a confidentiality agreement.

Tristan Derrington has a reputation for doing what he wants, when he wants. Usually nothing will stop Tristan from pursuing a gorgeous beauty like Logan, but even temptation in four-inch heels won't stand in the way of him finding his sister and exposing HCS. He may think he has a solid plan to avoid their obvious attraction, but even the best laid plans can fail. The more time they spend together, the harder it is to deny their explosive chemistry. Especially when they realize how delicious giving into temptation can be.

HIGH CLASS SOCIETY INTRODUCTION

In a society of trust fund babies, millionaires and upper-class peers, four women seeking a prestigious education were thrust into a privileged world of wealth and aristocrats. Overwhelmed by the segregation they witnessed in the university that forced students to date within their own social class, they decide to create a world not based on society's rules. An organization in which the everyday woman not given the chance to date a person of caliber can overcome the barriers placed before her and date whomever she pleases.

This may include an athlete, billionaire, chef or politician. There are no limits to finding love and they simply supply women the tools and encouragement to go after the person they want in hopes that it results in a successful relationship.

Hence, after graduating from Yale in 2006, High Class Society Incorporated was established. Now, years later, although all four founding women have established successful careers, the secret organization is in full effect. But like every secret society, the biggest obstacle is keeping it a secret.

HCS CODE OF ETHICS

i. In order to be a HCS member prospect, you must be invited by a founder or a member on the board of directors. Members may also suggest prospects, but cannot contact a prospect directly before HCS can review.

ii. HCS is a private organization and all women are sworn to secrecy.

iii. Unbeknownst to society, the HCS team works daily to build solid, well-researched profiles on eligible bachelors.

iv. Please be aware that we are not the typical matchmaking service. Once you take our rigorous personal, professional and spiritual assessment, you are placed in a position to meet quality matches.

v. Our diverse group of members are intelligent and sophisticated. Each woman is successful in her own way. No gold diggers/groupies allowed.

vi. Members will be registered using their fingerprint. All HCS files are available online only and accessible through unique identifiers.

vii. HCS is a family. Even after our members enter successful relationships, they continue to be a part of High Class Society.

viii. At HCS, we offer you the tools, encouragement and resources to be the best version of yourself. If you respect the process and believe in our mission, it truly works.

PROLOGUE

January 2006, Yale University

"THAT'S IT! I'm done wasting my time on these snobbish boys who think more with their wallets than their minds."

Logan Sapphire looked up from her notebook as her friend Harper Rose entered their apartment.

"I'm guessing the date didn't go well."

Harper huffed. "Let's try terrible. Horrible. Possibly the worst date of my entire life."

"Maybe you're forgetting about that frat guy you went out with two months ago," said their other roommate, Peyton Davis, as she entered the living room and took a seat on the chair opposite Logan. "If I remember correctly, he rushed your date because he had to take out that freshman and he actually had the nerve to tell you that."

"Oh right," Harper said as she kicked off her heels and plopped on the couch. "Yeah, he was pretty bad."

All three ladies glanced at the door as their fourth roommate, Savannah Westbrook, entered the apartment lugging a book bag, tote bag, and laptop bag that she immediately dropped at the entrance. Logan never did understand why Savannah always carried around so much stuff, but that was Savannah. She was always researching, studying, or doing something that required her to take her notes, books and laptop everywhere.

"What did I miss?" Savannah asked as she sat on the couch next to Harper.

Harper sighed. "Just me ranting about my sorry excuse for a date with that arrogant jerk I went out with tonight."

"Wait, isn't he that fine guy from your photo journalism class that you were dying to go out with? I thought he seemed different than the others."

"They're all the same," Harper replied. "Not only did he spend most the night talking about himself, his money, and his dad's company that he was going to be working at right after graduation. But then he had the nerve to slip me a key card for the hotel room he'd booked for the night."

"What did you tell him?" Logan asked. Harper was the insightful one in the group so there was no doubt in her mind that Harper tried to explain to him exactly why he was an arrogant jerk instead of just cursing him out. She was the one who didn't just take things from surface value, but instead, she always took a deeper look.

"He told me that most women would jump at the opportunity to have sex with him on a first date. So I told him all the reasons why he would never get into my panties."

"The nerve of these guys. See, this is the only reason why I regret not going to a regular university. There are some real pretentious assholes here," Peyton chimed in.

"And even if you're lucky enough to find a *trust fund* guy here who is actually decent, you run into issues with his friends and family accepting you," Logan added. Although she was currently engaged to one of those *privileged* men and had been dating him for most of college, she couldn't help that feeling in the pit of her stomach. That feeling that warned her she was making the wrong decision by marrying him after college and joining a family that didn't accept her or think she was worthy enough to carry their last name. She didn't date him for his money, but his family didn't see it that way.

"We aren't the only women with these issues," Savannah stated. "Just last week, I was talking to perky Paula, who couldn't stop crying in class after her boyfriend of three years broke up with her."

Logan shook her head in disbelief. "They were so in love. Please tell me it's not because her family had to file for bankruptcy."

"You guessed it," Savannah confirmed. "Apparently, being with someone who no longer has money isn't a good look. Three years down the drain."

"See, I worked my ass off to get here," Harper said. "Being from a low or middle-class family shouldn't make me less worthy of love than someone born from money. Isn't love about finding your soul mate and the person you want to spend the rest of your life with? Wouldn't you rather have a hardworking woman by your side, money or no money?"

Peyton leaned over and slapped hands with Harper. "Agreed. And the opening line on a date shouldn't be how much my family makes or how dating me can improve or decrease their social status."

Logan glanced around at her friends as they began sharing stories that they'd heard around campus from women who had fallen for a guy only to realize that because of social status, they couldn't be together. Logan and her roommates were all from hard-working families and each had worked hard to get accepted into Yale on scholarship and follow their dreams. They didn't major in the same discipline, but they'd instantly connected during freshman orientation week and had been close all through college. Even though it was their last semester, she was certain they would remain friends after graduation and already, the foursome was planning on moving to New York together.

"You know what's crazy," Logan said finally closing her notebook and placing it on the coffee table. "We each gained so much by attending Yale, but I think you all agree that we've never faced this much adversity when it came to dating and by the sound of it, there are so many ladies on campus that are in the same boat as we are. And not just here at Yale, I'm sure this is an issue outside of school as well."

Harper nodded her head in agreement. "I think you're right. My cousin went through a similar issue with liking a man she met at a business conference. She said he was really interested in her as well, but after spending the first two conference days together, he was pulled in several different directions by other women."

"So he just stopped talking to her?" Logan asked.

"Sort of. See, at her company she's an executive assistant, which is a great position and she really loves it. She accompanied the president of her company on the trip. But the women approaching the man she was interested in were all VP's, Presidents of other companies or women who were part of a family that sponsored the conference. Since his organization was planning the conference, his job as CEO of the event was to wine and dine all clients to try and get new business."

Logan began seeing the bigger picture. "So basically, he was interested, but because of obligations to talk to the other women, he couldn't spend as much time with her."

"That's right. But I told her that I felt like she should have

4

just continued to talk to him like she had been. She wasn't invited to every event at the conference, but she was invited to enough where she could have pushed past those women and made an effort."

"Easier said than done," Savannah said. "It's one thing to know a man is interested. It's another issue entirely to have the confidence not to care about what the other people in attendance think and convince yourself that you're bold enough to talk to him."

"I agree with Savannah," Peyton said. "Sometimes it's about self-confidence and the idea that you aren't any different than the other women vying for his attention. All men who have money or were born from money don't only want to date women from influential families. We run into that a lot here at Yale, but I guess we have to keep in mind that we are dealing with boys trying to be men. Not men who already know what they want and don't care about what others think."

"Those men are out there," Logan added with a sly smile. "We just have to find them."

Harper squinted her eyes at Logan. "Lo, I know that look. What are you thinking?"

"Do you guys remember last year when we were sitting around drinking wine after celebrating Savannah's twenty-first birthday?"

They all nodded their head in agreement. "Do you remember what we discussed that night?"

Savannah scrunched her head in thought. "Was that the time we stayed up all night discussing what it would be like in a world that didn't have typical dating rules that you had to follow? I think we talked about how it would be if we could date good men and not worry about whether or not money, family names, or social standing would be an issue."

"Exactly," Logan said snapping her fingers. "Peyton, you

said you would love it if we could start our own organization. Then Harper, you started talking about how great it would be if it were a secret organization that no one knew about. Then Savannah, you and I started talking about the way the organization could work and how great it would be if we also encouraged women to pursue love and help build their self-esteem. Especially if their self-esteem was damaged as a result of a bad relationship."

"Um, so what exactly are you getting at?" Peyton asked inquisitively. "Because it sounds a lot like you're trying to say we should turn the ideas we had that day into reality."

Logan smiled and clasped her hands together as she looked at each roommate.

"Oh no," Savannah said shaking her head. "That's precisely what you're trying to say isn't it?"

"Come on guys, you all have to admit that our ideas that night were pretty amazing."

"I'm pretty sure I was tipsy," Harper mentioned.

"No you weren't. We had just started drinking our first glass when we talked about this." Logan got up from her chair and began pacing the room as her brain began working overtime.

"Hear me out ladies. Peyton, you have amazing business sense and there is no doubt in my mind that you have what it takes to handle the ins and outs of a secret organization. Savannah, you're amazing at researching and like we discussed last year, it would be great if we could develop profiles of eligible bachelors, but they have to be the right type of men. Harper, you're a wiz with marketing and social media. Private or not, we will definitely need that. And of course, since I'm majoring in human resources, I could handle meeting and conversing with the members."

She turned and was greeted with blank stares from all three women, so she continued talking. "I know we would have to work out a lot of kinks and really solidify our business plan, but there is no doubt in my mind that we were on to something great the night of Savannah's birthday and I'm sure, if we put our minds to it, we could create something amazing. A secret society unlike any other."

When their faces still displayed blank stares, she'd thought maybe she was talking too fast and they hadn't heard her. She was relieved when Harper's mouth curled to the side in a smile.

"I can't believe I'm saying this, but I honestly loved the idea when we first came up with it last year, and I love it even more now that we're graduating. Off hand, I can already think about several women who would be more than happy to join."

"So, we're really going to do this?" Savannah said with a smile. "We are actually going to start our own secret society?"

"Not just any society," Peyton said as she stood to join Logan. "Didn't we create some guidelines for the organization that night?"

"I think I have all our notes from that," Logan said as she ran to her room to grab her laptop and returned to the living room. She kneeled down at the coffee table, opened up a word document, and was joined by Harper, Savannah and Peyton who kneeled down around her laptop as well.

"Here it is. All our notes from that night."

Savannah pointed to sentence. "Oh wow, it says here that we thought members should have to take a rigorous personal, professional and spiritual assessment when they join before they are placed in a position to meet quality matches."

Harper pointed to another sentence. "And here it says that we will build well-researched profiles on eligible bachelors and give women the tools and encouragement to go after the man of their dreams."

"So we decided that this wouldn't be a match making service right?" Peyton asked the group. "We would place women in a position to meet a man they are interested in, but we aren't playing matchmaker and setting them up on a date."

"That seems accurate to what we discussed," Logan answered. "But of course, we'll have to get all those details nailed down before inviting members."

"Didn't we come up with a name too?" Peyton asked searching the notes on the page.

Logan scrolled down until she landed on the page she was searching for.

"High Class Society Incorporated," she said aloud to the group. "That was the name we created last year."

Harper clasped her hands together. "Oh I remember now! I still love that name."

"Me too," Savannah and Peyton said in unison.

Logan pointed her finger to the words on the screen written underneath the name of the organization and read them aloud. "There are no limits to finding love, no rulebook to discover your soul mate, and no concrete path to follow in order to reach your destiny. In High Class Society, we make that journey a little easier. High Class Society ... where elite and ordinary meet."

She looked up at each of the ladies, each with a knowing gleam in their eyes. This year didn't just mark their graduation and start of their careers. It also marked the beginning of a new chapter for the four of them. A chapter that was sure to be filled with pages and pages of new self-discoveries

CHAPTER 1

$\mathcal{N}$*ine years later...*

"You have *one* minute to tell me where the hell my sister is, or I'll have no choice but to call the authorities and expose this disgraceful ass company."

The deep timbre in the man's voice bounced off the burgundy walls of the Manhattan office and teased Logan's ears. Her big, doe-eyes stared at the sexy intruder with the rich, mocha skin tone as she tried her best not to drop her mouth open in admiration. She knew who he was. Her company had done their research on him when Logan had first met his sister. They were actually in the process of gathering further information on him to build a more solid profile and add him to their list of exceptional men. However, the pictures definitely didn't do this former Canadian turned New Yorker justice.

In the profile she'd received from her partner and friend,

Savannah Westbrook, the Director of Research and Development for High Class Society, she could tell he was a walking sex ad. Even after recognizing his clearly masculine sex appeal, she couldn't have prepared herself for the onslaught of pleasure she'd feel coming face-to-face with temptation.

Her eyes wandered up and down the length of his body that was encased in a deep-blue Tom Ford suit, complementing leather shoes, and a classic navy-blue watch with gold trimmings. Licking her lips as she admired his six-foot frame, she tried not to imagine how enticing he'd look without a stitch of clothing on. Usually Logan was attracted to men with curly hair and a caramel complexion, but the man standing before her didn't have either of those qualities … and damned if she even cared. Within a few seconds, she'd dismissed every physical characteristic she'd ever believed she wanted in a man. *Delicious,* she thought after taking note of his short fade and chiseled jawline, his neatly groomed features mirroring that of a Tyson Beckford look-alike rather than Shemar Moore.

"I'm so sorry, Lo," said her assistant, Nina, a grad student at Columbia University, as she came rushing in to the office behind the unwelcomed guest. "I'm not sure how he even got clearance into the building or how he found your office."

"It wasn't hard to find your office with so few people here and a distracted security guard," he explained, his eyes never straying from Logan. His piercing gaze was so intense that Logan was glad she was sitting at her desk or she would have surely faltered. "And you should really lock up the bathroom window in the basement. I climbed right in."

She tilted her head to the side, unable to believe that a man of his status would climb through a window to get into their office.

"It's okay, Nina," she reassured, refusing to break their stare-down. "I'll listen to what Mr. Derrington has to say."

Nina hesitantly exited the office and left the door cracked, instead of closing it all the way like she normally would when Logan had a meeting.

"Ms. Sapphire, I take it that you already know who I am," he stated with a slight curl of his lips. *Don't do that,* she thought when he walked a little closer to her desk. His imposing stance was already sending her body into a frenzy. She couldn't stay seated and let him have the upper hand.

"It appears you already know who I am as well, Mr. Derrington." Rising from her seat, she noted the appreciative glance he shot in her direction. She smoothed out her designer skirt and blouse before sitting on the edge of her desk. His eyes ventured to her creamy, maple thighs before making their way to the swell of her breasts.

Logan's breath caught as she watched him observe her. She was hardly showing any cleavage and her clothes were concealing all of her assets. Yet the way he was staring at her, made her feel as if she wasn't wearing anything at all. The air around them was thick with awareness, and the silence almost caused her to fidget under his stare.

"I've been away on business and came back early because I hadn't heard from my younger sister. So I went to her condo, and imagine my surprise when I surfed her laptop, trying to find some information about her whereabouts, and saw several screen shots saved in a folder on her desktop entitled High Class Society Incorporated."

Logan winced at his statement, silently cursing his discovery. HCS prided themselves on being paperless, a key to keeping the organization a secret. Unfortunately, no matter how good their small IT team was, some things were hard to avoid ... like members taking screen shots containing information that couldn't get out to the public.

"Ms. Sapphire, after I got over the shock of an organization like yours existing, I researched the duties of the founders listed on one of the screen shots and realized that you may be the only person to know where my sister is. According to what I read, all women are supposed to check in daily with you if they're away with a prospect, correct?"

"That is true," Logan responded. "May I remind you that the contents on those screen shots are private, and my organization did not approve for your sister to go off on her own before finishing part two of her orientation session, including our policy on safety."

"So she *is* with a man," he said more to himself than her. His jaw twitched and he placed both hands in his pockets, frustration radiating from his body. "May I remind *you* that as long as my sister is missing, everything is my business. She wouldn't have gotten this idea to run off with God knows who if your company didn't exist."

"We help women find the person of their dreams, Mr. Derrington. We have rules, which she didn't follow. We aren't babysitters."

"I assume I don't need to reinforce that I'll sue you for all your worth if you don't tell me what I need to know, Ms. Sapphire ... if that's even your real last name."

"It is," she stated firmly. "I have nothing to hide, and although this is against my better judgment, I will tell you who she's with," she continued, purposely leaving out the fact that she didn't know where Sophia was. She did have something to hide, but she needed to bluff to buy her and her partners some time before he went to the authorities.

"So," he said, removing both hands from his pockets and waving them for her to explain, "who is my sister with?"

Logan sighed, still not okay with sharing the information, but she knew he wasn't leaving without an answer. "She's with social media prodigy, Justice Covington."

She watched all of the color drain from his face while

both hands curled into fists. His breathing grew heavier and he slowly rolled his neck ... purposeful ... measured. Logan found her own breathing growing labored as she sat and watched a range of emotions cross his face.

"Then we definitely have a problem," he stated as he released his fists and leaned in closer to her, "because Justice Covington met my sister when she was eighteen and they tried to get married two years ago. If we don't find them, he may finally get his wish ... *if* they haven't tied the knot already."

* * *

30 MINUTES EARLIER ...

"WHERE ARE YOU?" Logan Sapphire asked aloud as she scrolled through the online files she had for one of the newest clients to High Class Society, Sophia Derrington. Her cherry-colored office desk—that was usually extremely organized—was covered in an array of paperwork and maps she'd printed to try and piece together where Sophia might be. In all of her eight years of being Director of HR and Recruiting, she'd never lost contact with a client for this long.

"What the hell am I going to do?" she huffed aloud, standing up and running her French tipped fingernails through her thick and wavy copper-colored hair. She paced back and forth in her office, glad that her partners had all retired for the night. Only Logan and her assistant remained, and she was extremely thankful that Nina had decided to help her search for Sophia, despite the fact that Nina felt partially responsible.

Sophia hadn't been born from wealth, but thirty-four-year-old Tristan Derrington, Sophia's older brother, was a self-made millionaire and one of the most sought after custom watch designers in the country. He created top-notch designs for numerous celebrities, singers, hip-hop artists, and political figures. High Class Society had certain rules, and one of them was to ensure that the only women allowed in the society were women who weren't born from money or from highly privileged families. They were all successful professionals and entrepreneurs, or self-made millionaires. Of course, sometimes rules were meant to be broken, and in some instances, they made an exception and allowed a woman to join who was born from money or a well-known family. Those situations were handled on a case-by-case basis.

Even though it seemed unfair, Logan and her partners had strict rules that they had to adhere to in order to ensure that High Class Society was successful and effective. They didn't just let any woman into the organization. Each woman went through a psychological, spiritual, and professional screening to ensure that they were truly looking for love and not a gold-digging groupie. Their clientele consisted of women of different nationalities, ethnic backgrounds, and occupations, and they were proud of the successful relationships that had developed from their company.

Logan stopped pacing and abruptly sat down in her desk chair, accidentally knocking over a cup of black coffee as she did so. "Shit," she cursed, quickly grabbing some nearby napkins and dabbing up the coffee.

"Are you okay?" Nina yelled from outside of her office.

"I'm fine," she yelled back after she'd wiped up most of the coffee and waved the wet stained paperwork in the air to dry it quicker.

Focus, Logan! she thought to herself as she leaned back in her chair and clasped her hands in her lap. *Are there any clues in the last conversation you had with Sophia?*

Ever since she'd first met Sophia months ago, the twenty-four year old had wormed her way into Logan's heart after divulging the story about how she'd lost the only man she had ever loved and was ready to see what else was out there. She'd claimed she needed High Class Society, and Logan had chosen to ignore the signs that something more was going on. Now that she had no idea where Sophia had run off to, she had time to reflect on the fact that Sophia had only shown interest in one man ... Justice Covington. HCS always listed possible matches in each woman's personal online folder and Sophia had included other men in her profile as "persons of interest," but any time Logan had spoken with Sophia, the young lady had only asked her about Justice, the thirty-two-year-old brain behind an up and coming social media network.

Closing her eyes, she thought back to the information she'd given Sophia about Justice attending a Broadway play at the Ethel Barrymore Theatre here in New York. She had warned Sophia to focus on men closer to her own age, but she'd been determined to meet Justice. That was the last day they'd spoken almost two weeks ago. Since then, she'd only received one text from Sophia saying that she was okay and was following her heart. All of their HCS ladies knew they had to check in daily if they were going away with a man, so she was worried and pissed that Sophia was jeopardizing the company and going rogue.

"What am I missing?" she wondered aloud before going on her computer to look at the personal file they had on Justice Covington again. There was a reason Sophia was interested in Justice, and why Savannah hadn't been able to track Justice's whereabouts lately in regards to his relationship status. Something wasn't adding up.

"Sir, you can't go in there," she heard Nina yell right before a man walked into her office, literally taking her breath away. *Tristan Derrington ... in the flesh.* God, he was sexy. Although she wished she could relish in his presence, the fact that he was standing in her office meant that HCS was in more trouble than she knew.

CHAPTER 2

*L*ogan could usually put on a great bluff, but right now, shock was splashed across her face. She always prided herself on being able to predict when something would happen before it happened, but she definitely hadn't predicted this.

Last year, Forbes magazine had done an article on top professionals under thirty to watch out for, and she'd been elated when they had asked her to do an interview. Although she was now thirty years of age, being Vice President of Human Resources for one of the largest beauty retailers in the United States meant that her hard work and success had paid off way earlier than expected. When asked how she remained so calm under stress, she told them that she never made a decision without fully thinking out every outcome. Therefore, she was always prepared for the rewards or consequences of her decisions.

As she stared at Tristan, barely able to close her mouth, she realized that her answer to that question last year was no longer a viable response.

"I'm sorry, but I'm not sure I heard you correctly." She

cleared her throat before continuing. "Did you just say that Justice Covington tried to marry Sophia two years ago?"

Tristan braced his arms over her desk and leaned closer toward her, the hint of Tom Ford's Private Blend Lavender Palm cologne teasing her nostrils. *Good lawd!* She'd bet any dollar amount that the man standing before her matched all his suit brands with the scent of his cologne.

Instead of backing further into her desk chair, she remained still, mesmerized by the tingles traveling throughout her body at their closeness. She hadn't felt those tingles in months, and she hated that she still missed the last guy who had made her weak in the knees. She couldn't even call him an ex-boyfriend, more like a weekly booty call, but nevertheless, he still invaded her thoughts at the most inappropriate moments.

"That's precisely what I'm saying," Tristan stated firmly. "And if I know my sister, she's probably making plans to tie the knot as we speak."

Oh shit. She hated to admit it to herself, but she wasn't prepared for the outcome of this situation. It seemed like every conclusion she imagined in her head painted High Class Society in a negative light.

"I can fix this," she replied, trying to stall for more time.

"And how do you propose to do that?" he inquired, finally leaning up from her desk. She appreciated the small distance he'd placed between them ... even though without his imperial presence looming over her, she still couldn't think of a good solution to the problem.

Silence filled the confines of the office and the expression on Tristan's face let her know that his patience was wearing thin. He opened his mouth to say something to her when his phone dinged. He quickly pulled the device from his pocket to view the cause of the chime.

"She finally turned her phone back on," he said with

relief. "I had a tracking device put in her phone last year. Didn't know it would come in handy so soon. "

Logan released the breath she had been holding as Tristan began taping buttons on his phone. He was concentrating intently on whatever he was typing and anticipation was starting to get the best of her.

"Well," Logan got up for her desk to stand in front of him, "where is she?"

"She's entering Utah soon," he stated, never looking up from his phone. *Utah? Oh no, I wonder if ...*

"She isn't heading to Vegas if that's what you're thinking," Tristan said reading her thoughts.

"Well that's good," Logan exclaimed. "Are you texting her right now?"

He briefly glanced up from his phone to glare at her before returning his eyes to his phone. "Not that it's any of your business, but I just told her that I know everything about this organization and demanded she return home and not think for a second about marrying Justice."

"The moment you stormed into my office it became my business," she snapped as she placed one arm on her hip and threw his words back at him. "Besides, we don't even know if they are getting married. Plus, if you think telling a twenty-four-year-old woman not to do something will make her not do it, then you obviously don't know women very well."

"I know enough," he replied, still typing away on his phone.

"Well what makes you so sure she isn't heading to Vegas?"

She expected to see the same stern expression on Tristan's face when he looked at her, but instead of frustration reflecting in his eyes, there was sadness. The look made her breath catch, and she wished they'd met under different circumstances so she could say something that would ease the sadness.

"I'm pretty sure she's taking a road trip to Napa Valley, California."

Logan waited for him to continue before finally realizing that he wasn't going to go into any more details. She was relieved that they knew where Sophia was, and now it seemed that the biggest obstacle she was facing was the fact that she had to convince Tristan not to expose their company. *Maybe he would understand what we do if he knew a little more about us instead of what's portrayed on those screen shots he saw?* She knew getting him to understand was a long shot, but she had to at least try.

"So," Logan muttered as she shuffled from one heel to the other. "Now that we know where she is, and you seem to know where she is headed, it seems we will soon have this situation under control."

He gave a slight laugh before responding. "Your problems are far from over. I still think this company is a disgrace, and the fact that you try to manipulate the way people fall in love by telling a woman where a rich guy will be and the best way to snag him is unethical on so many levels. Prying on the insecurities of needy women or recruiting the ultimate groupie and posing her as a woman of quality is barbaric."

Say what! "There's nothing barbaric about the way we conduct business, Mr. Derrington. I assure you, our women aren't needy or groupies looking to land a rich husband or wife depending on their interests." There had been a couple times that someone had found out about their business, and her and the other three founders had to smooth things over and explain the details of High Class Society, not to mention, loop in their amazing lawyer. However, never had their organization been called barbaric.

"And in my eyes, you're the worst of them all," he said, completely ignoring her statement. "I noticed the job titles of the founders on one of the screen shots, and since you are the Director of HR and Recruitment, you're the one who actually invites women to join this organization. How do you even sleep at night knowing you're deceiving so many people? You can't possibly believe you're making a positive difference."

Who the hell does he think he is? Normally, Logan would never tolerate such disrespect and words never failed her, but she didn't know what type of man Tristan Derrington was. Plus, she really couldn't afford to piss him off too much to the point where he really did turn them over to the authorities. They weren't breaking any laws, but the organization wasn't exactly the easiest to explain to people. To the women who were a part of the organization, their methods were definitely considered ethical because they all shared a commonality in the sense that they truly believed in HCS's mission. Yet there was no doubt in Logan's mind that people, men in particular, would try to get the organization shut down if they found out about HCS.

"Listen clearly, Mr. Derrington," she said, stepping closer to him and crossing her hands in front of her. It was either that, or wring his neck to rid herself of the irritation seething through her body. "We don't deceive women. We offer them hope and possibilities. Encouragement and reassurance. I don't expect a man like you to agree with everything we do here, but I do demand respect when you're standing in my office."

She had his full attention, but he didn't say anything. "I've spent years being judged by people like you ... men who turn their noses up at something they don't understand and pass judgment without a second glance. I've had to overcome a lot of adversity. So," she began, taking another step forward to make sure he heard every word, "I need you to get off that throne you've placed yourself on and address me like a

SHERELLE GREEN

respectful woman ... not the barbarian your senile ass thinks I am."

* * *

TRISTAN BLINKED at the brown-eyed beauty frowning at him and tried his best not to drop his gaze to her cappuccino-colored lips. They appeared soft and inviting ... so unlike her overall defensive stance that was guarded and frustrated.

He didn't care that he'd pissed her off because he was pretty damn pissed himself. To think that there were women who ran a secret organization like this was infuriating for a man like him who spent most of his days avoiding gold-digging, loose women with no morals ... something that came with the territory when working with people in the entertainment industry. Whatever happened to people pursuing a relationship just for the sake of falling in love, and not for the desire to get ahead in life through money, greed, and power?

When he'd first arrived home from his business trip, gone to his sister's condo, and discovered the High Class Society screen shots on her laptop, he'd only performed a quick Google search of the names he'd found before rushing over to the address of the building that was scribbled on a piece of paper near Sophia's computer. During his drive to the building, he'd almost gotten into an accident when he researched the founders. He was shocked to find out that each woman had numerous articles written about her, and each had successful careers. The minute he'd landed on Logan's picture, he'd felt a kick in his gut at his instant attraction. However, seeing a picture of her online didn't compare to the temptation standing in front of him right now.

"I guess I just expected more from a Yale graduate," he finally said, unable to resist annoying her even more. When she opened her mouth to speak again, he lifted his hand and cut her off. "But maybe I'm not being completely fair. You didn't start this company on your own. Must take a really fucked up group of women to come up with a place like High Class Society."

"How dare you?" she yelled in a frustrated huff as she scrunched her forehead. With a swiftness that Tristan hadn't been expecting, her right hand lifted and landed directly on his left cheek in one loud smack.

"You arrogant ass, I've never been so disrespected in my life," she shouted.

At that moment, her assistant peeked her head into the room. "Is everything okay?"

"It will be once this egotistical a-hole leaves my office." She took a step back from him.

"The truth hurts, doesn't it?" he taunted. At his words, Logan's hand began lifting again, but Tristan instantly caught her wrist to avoid another smack.

The moment their skin connected, he felt it ... that rare feeling of unadulterated awareness. And from the gasp he heard escape her stunning lips, she felt it, too. He studied her light brown eyes, unable to say anything. Two seconds ago, she had been ready to smack the shit out of him. Now, she seemed to be having a hard time tearing her eyes away from him.

Her scent, which had been driving him insane with need since he'd arrived, filled the office. Why in the world did he have to be so attracted to a woman that represented everything he hated in the opposite sex? The only thing worse than being attracted to a woman he knew he should stay away from was resisting the urge to kiss her senseless.

"Come with me to help me find my sister," he demanded without thinking, still lightly gripping her wrist.

"Absolutely not." Her eyes left his and went to her wrist.

He followed her eyes, noticing for the first time that his thumb was rubbing her skin in small circles.

"If you do," he began, pulling her slightly closer to him, "I'd be willing to listen to your explanation of this unusual organization." He left out any key descriptive words that would have ticked her off. The slight lift of her eyebrows proved she was entertaining the idea.

"If I go," she said finally, removing her wrist from his grasp, "you have to promise to sign a confidentiality agreement."

"Hell no," he replied with a stern laugh.

"Then we don't have a deal," she said as she looked at her assistant. "Nina, can you please walk Mr. Derrington out."

The assistant began making her way to him, and he knew it was for the better. No telling what they may have done had her assistant not walked into the room. Tristan was known for always thinking with his head and not the lower part of the male anatomy, but seduction in stilettos was making him throw caution to the wind.

"Okay," Tristan acquiesced when her assistant had reached him. "How about you come with me to find my sister, and I'll agree to a meeting between our lawyers to review the confidentiality agreement?"

There was no way his lawyer would agree for him to sign that document, and the moment he'd discovered High Class Society, he knew that no matter what, he would bring down the organization. However, he didn't see any reason why he couldn't enjoy Logan's company before he ousted her and the other founders.

Squinting her eyes, she studied his face. After a few more seconds of silence, she seemed to have made a decision.

"You win, Mr. Derrington," she responded with a sigh. "I'll go with you to find your sister."

He didn't even bother to stop the sly smile that crept onto

his face. "Good," he said, clasping his hands together as he prepared to depart. "We leave tomorrow morning at 10 a.m. I already have your contact info, so I'll have a car pick you up from here at the office."

He saw her mouth drop open right before he turned around. She couldn't possibly have believed he wouldn't leave right away. Hell, he would have left tonight if he thought he could get his pilot and crew together for his private plane in time.

As he was leaving the office, he heard Logan's assistant ask her if she was okay. He couldn't hear her answer, but he knew she wasn't okay given that he'd discovered her company. *Too bad I have to bring down someone so sexy.* And he had no doubt he would find out just how sexy Logan Sapphire really was.

CHAPTER 3

*S*he was so screwed. Royally screwed. Even worse, she had no idea how she would get herself out of this mess. High Class Society was in real jeopardy and she wasn't stupid, Tristan had no plan to have their lawyers meet or sign the confidentiality agreement. He'd been acting like a complete ass the entire time he was in her office yesterday, until their skin had made contact. She'd bet any dollar amount that lust had been the sole deciding factor when he asked her to accompany him on the search for his sister. He'd felt it. She'd felt it. And by the look on Nina's face after Tristan had left, she had felt it, too.

Unfortunately, she couldn't decline his offer because there was always a chance that hearing the story behind the organization would resonate with him. After telling Nina to keep the encounter with Tristan and the fact that Sophia was missing between them, she'd called her friends to tell them that she had to unexpectedly handle business out of town. She often traveled for her full-time job, so none of the women thought it was unusual for an unexpected trip to happen. Then she'd called her job and told them that she had a family emergency. According to Tristan's email, he planned for them to be gone no longer than a couple days, but she had to cover all of her bases just in case. She didn't plan on facing her partners until she had something remotely positive to tell them when she broke the news.

"We're here, ma'am," the driver said, breaking her from her reverie as they pulled into an air landing at the municipal airport just outside of New York City. When the driver opened the door, she stepped out into the cold winter air and shivered as she looked at the stairs leading into the plane.

"Oh my," she murmured as she observed the size of the private plane. The details in his email also stated that they would be taking his plane for their search and rescue trip, but she'd expected something a lot smaller than what she was currently looking at.

She glanced at the driver, who had removed her medium-sized Louis Vuitton luggage from the trunk, and followed him to the plane. Her heel boots clicked on the ground surface lightly covered by a soft white blanket of snow. As she watched another man load her bag into the plane, she felt a wave a quivers travel throughout her entire body … and the cause was not the fact that it was only thirty degrees outside.

She peeked at the reason for her discomfort, and cursed her body for its reaction at the thought of him. Looking away from his piercing stare, she closed her eyes and took a deep breath. "This is ridiculous," she mumbled to herself quietly. She had to pull herself together and remember why she had even agreed to this insane trip in the first place.

Mustering up all of the indifference she could, she plastered on a fake smile and ascended the stairs of the plane.

"Glad you actually showed up," Tristan said to her as she passed him to enter the aircraft. There was no way she was going to stand outside and wait for his permission to enter.

"Contrary to what you believe, Mr. Derrington, I am a

woman of my word." She stopped short when she entered the plane, taken aback by its beauty. Crème leather seats, stocked bar, small fridge, a platter of fruit, cheese and crackers, two televisions, recliner seats, twin bed in corner, rich mahogany wood … this plane had all the luxury comforts of a five star hotel, not to mention, the element of seduction with the smooth R&B music playing in the background.

Tristan walked up behind her and whispered softly in her ear, "Let's drop the formalities." The heat from his mouth played with her lobe and her heart rate increased. She hadn't been seduced in a long time, and quite frankly, there had only been one man worth remembering anyway. All the others had been men to pass the time.

"I think formalities are necessary to keep ourselves focused on finding your sister," Logan said, her eyes glued straight ahead. She couldn't, *wouldn't* turn to face him. He didn't speak right away, and it was straight torture feeling his even breathing move from her ear to her neck. She clenched her vaginal muscles and tried to ease the tension that was slowly building in her core. At least she'd chosen to wear dark jeans and a white blouse rather than the black business dress she was originally going to wear. No doubt the extra fabric was making her feel more protected against his advances than a dress would have.

"I have my priorities in order," he said. She let out a soft moan and swore she felt the tip of his tongue touch the side of her neck. "So, do you prefer Logan or Lo?"

She took one long blink and chanced turning around to face him. When she did, his teasing smile proved he knew he had her. He looked much more casual today in jeans, a New York Yankees hoodie, and of course a stylish watch that she'd bet was one of his own custom designs. But the clothes did nothing to hide his incredibly sexy looks. If anything, it gave him a street edge that she hadn't seen the day before. Logan was a sucker for a successful and educated man born and raised in the streets, and from talking to his sister about her upbringing in Canada, she knew Tristan fit that profile.

"Either name is fine," she said, finally giving up. "What about you?"

"Tristan is fine, but I'm willing to let you call me Mr. Derrington, depending on the way you're screaming my name."

She caught herself before her eyes widened in shock. *Let me?* "I'm not some dog who will do whatever you want when you want. And I won't be screaming your name unless it's to put your conceited ass in place and bring your ego down a notch."

"We'll see," he said before walking over to take a seat. She stole a glance at his nice, firm butt and silently cursed at herself for being so weak.

Yup, royally screwed was definitely an accurate observation, she thought as she watched him buckle his seatbelt and take out his iPad.

"You may want to take a seat," he said, glancing over to her. "We're taking off soon."

"Duly noted, Mr. Derrington." She purposely tried to piss him off by addressing him formally, but the smile he gave her was anything other than annoyed. *Was he intrigued? Yes. Entertained? Yes. Annoyed? Definitely not.* She just added another item to her agenda: figure out what made Tristan Derrington lose his cool façade.

* * *

"Oh, Joshua, stop. You're too much."

Logan's laugh filled the plane, and for the third time in the past hour, Tristan wished he wasn't so annoyed by the

SHERELLE GREEN

fact that she was blatantly flirting with his impressionable, twenty-one-year-old flight attendant.

That's it. I'm only staffing female flight attendants from now on. As Tristan typed away on his iPad, he tried his best to refrain from stealing another glance at Logan's hand placed on Joshua's arm. Even more annoying was the look of accomplishment written on Joshua's face and the smug glances he shot Tristan's way. Luckily, one stern look at the young man made him stop the charade instantly.

They had been flying for about three hours and Logan had yet to say more than a few words to him. Yet she had plenty to say to his staff, pilot, and co-pilot.

"You're too sweet, Joshy," Logan said playfully. "I'm sure any young lady closer to your own age would be happy to date you."

"You are so sweet," Tristan repeated under his breath in a mocking tone.

"Did you say something?" Logan asked him with a raised eyebrow.

"I sure didn't," he lied, knowing she had already heard him.

"It sounded like you did," she sputtered back.

"Well, I can assure you that I didn't," he returned, shooting her a stern, yet teasing, glance. The soft curl of her lips let him know she was enjoying the banter, which was good since that seemed to be all that they did since they'd met.

Tristan refused to break the stare and it appeared that Logan had the exact same idea. In his peripheral, he noticed Joshua glancing from him to Logan, seemingly observing the unstated eye dual they were having. Just to show the young buck a thing or two about respecting one's territory, he broke the dual for a few seconds to allow his true desires of everything he wanted to do to Logan penetrate through his eyes.

Her gaze went from surprised to intrigued, then downright lustful as she took his challenge and allowed some naughty thoughts of her own to reflect through her eyes. He didn't break from Logan to peer at Joshua, but he felt Joshua's eyes on him.

"Rule number one, Joshua," Tristan said licking his lips at the thoughts still floating in Logan's gaze. "Don't let a woman like Logan suck you into her lady web with flirtatious comments and soft touches when she is obviously trying to make another man jealous. In the end, you will always look like the fool."

Logan tilted her head to the side and squinted her eyes together. "Rule number two, Joshua," she said with a slight smirk. "Women of today are only doing what men have been doing for centuries. In your position, the key to you winning this game is to pretend the other man doesn't exist because only the cocky and arrogant assume they are the only ones in the room worth anyone's attention."

When Logan broke eye contact to look at Joshua, so did Tristan.

"Also, make sure that you aren't making it too obvious that you realize the situation like you did with Tristan and I," Logan continued. "A woman likes a man who is so focused on her that others can't help but be jealous, rather than a man who is so focused on making others jealous that it isn't really about her at all."

After one more glance at both of them, Joshua shook his head and walked to the back of the plane. Tristan hated to admit it, but he liked the spin-off rule that Logan had stated.

The conversation, or rather the lack of, was halted when the co-pilot walked in and addressed Tristan.

"We have to stop in Denver, Colorado at the Denver

International Airport," the co-pilot said. "The snowstorm is too bad for us to continue, and all small planes have been advised to stop at the next airport and wait it out."

"How far would that push us back?" Tristan asked. He was so wrapped up in Logan that he'd chosen to ignore the turbulence until now.

"We hope not long, but the weather report shows another snowstorm approaching after this one passes. Between both storms, we may be able to leave for California tomorrow evening at the earliest."

"But it could be longer?" The co-pilot nodded his head. "Damn," he huffed aloud.

"You okay?" Logan asked in concern.

Tristan took another glance at his iPad to view the tracker for his sister. "She's still in Utah and I wanted to arrive in California before she did."

"Maybe the storm will slow them down, too."

"It won't," Tristan said, tapping his iPad. "Sophia is a Derrington, which means she's determined as hell. She won't let the weather stop her, but then again, I won't either."

"What do you mean?" Logan asked uneasily.

"It means," finalizing his payment, Tristan turned his iPad toward Logan, "the rental car I just reserved for us better maneuver great in the snow because it looks like our flight to Cali just turned into a winter road trip."

CHAPTER 4

*J*t's one thing to have the entire plane crew tell you that you're crazy. It's even worse when the manager of the car rental company would rather give you a refund than give you the car that you have already reserved.

"I didn't sign on for a death wish," Logan said as the click of her boots echoed throughout the parking garage, her luggage trailing behind. "I really think you need to reconsider driving to California in this snowstorm."

"We've already been through this," Tristan explained, not slowing his stride. "The deal is off if you don't accompany me on this road trip."

"You're insane," she replied as they arrived to the SUV Tristan had rented. "I agreed to a short trip to find your sister, but it's going to take us two days to get there in this storm."

"Eighteen hours is the normal driving distance from where we are, so in the storm, it should take at most a day, not two. Plus, I plan on driving throughout the night so I'm shooting for twenty hours." He hit the unlock button on the car remote and opened the passenger door.

Logan observed his outreached hands motioning for her to get in the vehicle, but she remained stationed right outside of the door. "I changed my mind," she crossed her arms over her chest, "I don't think this is a good idea. I'll stay in Denver and meet you in California when the storm clears."

"Here we go again." Raising his hands into the air, Tristan asked, "Are you always this difficult?" He left the passenger door open and grabbed their luggage before placing both in the trunk.

"Only when prompted." Logan expected him to come back to the passenger side of the door after he closed the trunk, but instead, he went to the driver's side and hopped in.

"Unbelievable," she huffed as her arms remained crossed.

"What do you expect me to do? Beg you to come with me? Because I'm not a beggar."

"And I don't listen to rude ass men who give me ultimatums." She didn't expect him to beg, but she was irritated at his constant dismissal of her opinion.

Dropping her head back, she heaved a big sigh. In her mind, she weighed her pros and cons. On one hand, she still believed that his plan to drive through a massive snowstorm to find his sister—who was probably having the time of her life—was completely and utterly ridiculous. On the other hand, it warmed her heart a little to see him so concerned about the well-being of his younger sister. Logan was the same with her sisters, and would move mountains to make sure they were okay.

When she brought her head back down, her eyes collided with his before she could avert them to another less attractive body part. After a slow perusal of his face and quick skim of his muscled body beneath his clothing, she concluded that Tristan Derrington probably didn't have an ugly bone in his body.

"Change your mind?" he asked when her gaze had settled on his lips.

LOGAN TOOK A CONSIDERABLY long blink before responding. "I guess." Hopping into the car, she quickly shut the door before she changed her mind yet again. "Let's just get this road trip started."

"I knew you'd make the right decision." Tristan started the engine and the car jumped to life.

"Cocky much," Logan replied as she buckled her seatbelt. His reply was a sly smirk that proved her point. Rolling her eyes, she shook her head. "This is going to be the longest road trip of my life."

As they left the parking garage and entered the sea of soft white flakes, she knew her last statement was the absolute truth.

* * *

FIVE HOURS INTO THE DRIVE, Logan had to admit that so far it wasn't as bad as she'd thought. With the exception of a stop at a gas station, they hadn't said more than a few words to one another since leaving the Denver airport, but she actually enjoyed the comfortable silence.

She leaned her head back in the seat and closed her eyes for the first time since their journey began. Logan wasn't one to dwell on past decisions, yet she couldn't help but think about her current circumstances as a result of her ignoring her gut.

When Sophia Derrington, their youngest HCS member, had come to Logan begging to be a part of High Class Society, Logan's first response had been a solid *NO!* To be a member of High Class Society, you had to be invited, and even though they accepted suggestions from members, the members were instructed never to approach a possible recruit until the HCS team could do a little research on that woman.

Her assistant, Nina, had met Sophia in one of their graduate classes, and they'd been placed on an assignment together. During one of their study sessions, Nina had logged into her HCS account to get some work done for Logan and didn't notice Sophia peeking at her screen. The next week, Sophia had cornered Nina and demanded to know about the organization after unsuccessfully searching the Internet for information.

After a few more weeks of questioning, Nina let it slip that it was a secret organization that helped women find love and confessed her lapse in judgment to Logan. Logan had immediately gone into action; the two met with Sophia the next day to try and smooth things over. She hadn't expected Sophia to beg to be a member. It seemed only fitting to make an exception and let Sophia join in exchange for her secrecy. Besides, she had grown quite found of her.

Logan slowly opened her left eye to glimpse at her vehicle companion. *If you had just followed your gut, you wouldn't even be in this situation right now,* she thought for the umpteenth time.

"Is there a reason why you're staring at me?"

She opened her other eye at the sound of Tristan's voice. "I was just thinking about how much you and Sophia look alike," she claimed.

"Well, she's much prettier than I am."

"That's probably the most selfless thing you've said since we met."

He raised one eyebrow at her. "Give me time," he replied with a smile. "I'm sure in an hour I'll be back to saying selfish things."

Logan's soft laugh echoed throughout the car. "So Mr. Serious does have a sense of humor."

"I have my moments," he said with a shrug. She wondered if she would get to see any other sides of his personality on this unplanned trip. She didn't know much about Tristan besides what she'd read in articles, and now that he'd discovered HCS, not only was Savannah probably not going to be able to create a profile for him, but also the future of HCS lingered in his hands.

Logan peered out the front window at the large snowflakes that were beginning to fall faster than they had hours prior. The view of the burnt orange sun setting in the distance over a mountain draped in white snow was breathtaking, but the worsening weather was beginning to make her nervous.

"Tell me more about yourself," she stated.

"What for?" Tristan asked with a laugh. "This trip is strictly business."

She winkled her forehead. "Because the weather is getting worse, and if something happens to us, I want to at least know more about you than your first and last name."

Tristan glanced at her before turning his eyes back to the road. "Why don't you start first?"

"Because this road trip was your idea, but if you aren't going to talk, how about we play the radio game?"

"What the hell is the radio game?"

Logan smiled before turning in her seat to face him. "In the radio game, you ask the radio a question and then scan the stations. The first song you hear is the answer to your question."

"Um, okay," Tristan replied questionably. "You made this game up?"

"Of course not." She waved her hand in the air. "I saw it back in the day on one of those popular TV shows."

"Oh in that case, we definitely need to play the radio game," Tristan said sarcastically.

She ignored his comment. "I'll go first. Is Tristan going to keep an open mind when I explain what HCS is all about?"

Tristan huffed as Logan scanned the station. She yelped in excitement when the song that played through the car speakers had the word *maybe* in the lyrics.

"Maybe is better than no. Now it's your turn."

Tristan scrunched his forehead and stole a glance in Logan's direction. *Oh lord, what is he thinking?*

He cleared his throat as a cunning smile spread across his face. "Will Logan be able to resist my charm on this trip, or will she listen to her body's need to get more intimately acquainted?"

As his hand made its way to the radio, Logan stopped him right before he hit the scan button. "That's more than one question and I thought we were keeping this PG."

"That was PG," he said, giving up the fight and glancing at the steering wheel instead. "I could have worded that question a whole lot worse."

"Crap," she whispered when she realized he could control the radio by using the buttons on the steering wheel. When the scan finally landed on a song, the words *kiss* and *touch* were easy to catch.

"That doesn't count," she quickly pointed out. "The song didn't really answer either of your questions."

"Oh yes it did," he said with a laugh. "And I got the message loud and *clear*."

The way his voice had dropped an octave or two was enough to make her stomach do a backwards flip in her seat. When he looked back over to her and caught her gaze, he allowed his intentions to show through his eyes the same way he had when they had been on the plane.

She didn't know what it was about this man, but being

around him felt dangerous. Like she wasn't sure if she should entertain his flirting or run in the opposite direction. Men often described her as sassy and outspoken, and although she had utilized her quick wit a few times with Tristan, she couldn't believe the times when her mind drew a blank. How could you know someone for only a day and feel like you've known that person much longer?

Her eyes were so locked to his, that she almost didn't notice two sets of red and blue lights flickering out of the corner of her eye.

"Look out!" she yelled as her head whipped toward the front of the car window. Tristan stopped the car within inches of the male police officer that was clearly not too happy with how fast he was driving in the snow.

"Hello, officer," Tristan said after he pressed the button to roll down his window.

"Son, do you have any idea how dangerous it is to be driving in his snowstorm?"

"Yes, I understand, but we have a family emergency and we have to get to California as soon as possible."

The officer began shaking his head. "You're not going any farther than this point tonight. The bridge ahead is covered in black ice and there have already been two minor accidents."

"I understand," Tristan responded. "We'll enter the address in the GPS and take another route."

"No need. All roads are blocked, and the other expressway is at a standstill. We are advising all patrons to get off at this exit, make a right, and head two miles down the road to the inn located on your left." The officer waved them toward the exit.

Reluctantly, Tristan thanked the officer and made his way to the exit. Logan let out a small chuckle and didn't stop when Tristan turned to glare at her.

"Guess sometimes we all have to do what we're told," she stated, feeding his irritation. She didn't mind staying at an inn for the night and getting out of this terrible snowstorm.

Tristan remained quiet the entire short commute to the inn. Once they made their way through the tiny lobby and to the registration desk, he finally spoke to ask about room reservations.

"Sorry, folks, all of our rooms are booked for the night," said the man standing behind the counter with a shirt way too tight and a baseball cap a little too dirty.

"You can't be serious," Tristan said. "A police officer sent us here."

"As he did every other car who came to that intersection before you."

"What about another inn?"

"In this storm? Good luck. There isn't another place to stay for over ten miles, and with the roads blocked, you wouldn't get there anyway."

"So what are we supposed to do?" Logan asked. At first she enjoyed seeing Tristan get aggravated, but now she needed resolutions.

"Hey? Are you that watch guy?" an excited voice questioned from behind them. Logan and Tristan turned to see a man and woman approaching them wearing matching green coats that had the words *The Mountain Moose* written on the front of them.

"Um, watch guy?" Tristan asked.

"Yeah, that watch guy I seen on that talk show," the man explained. "You design those watches for those celebrities."

"Ahh," Tristan said, nodding his head. "Guilty as charged."

"Well slap me two times and call me Susie, I knew it was you."

What the hell? Who were these people and why did she get

the feeling that their night would be one she would never forget.

"Take a picture, hunny," the man demanded, gripping Tristan for the photo opp. Logan laughed a little when Tristan ducked his head and successfully avoided two pictures. She wasn't sure why, but she figured she'd ask him later.

"Maybe next time," the man said, waving off his wife. "I'm Ed. My wife and I were planning on getting a room since the mechanic shop is closed and our heat is broken in our RV. But just like they told you, no rooms are available. We have two bedrooms in the RV, though, and we stay in the master room. If you don't mind being too cold, you could stay in the second bedroom. We come to these mountains and inn all the time, but we never met a celebrity. We'd love to tell all our friends in Oklahoma that you stayed in our RV."

"Oh, that would be so lovely," the woman exclaimed, clapping her hands together. "They call me chatty Kathy although my name is actually Catherine, but my parents figured that Kathy fit better with the word chatty and coined the nickname chatty Kathy. So there you have it. Chatty Kathy here to chat you up whenever you need chatting."

Logan and Tristan turned their heads to each other at the exact same time, each laughing along with the couple, but truly laughing only to mask how uncomfortable they felt.

"Um, well …" As Tristan's words broke off, Logan prayed that he wasn't about to agree to stay in an RV with strangers. "I guess we can take a look at the RV," he continued.

"You just made our night," the couple said as they ushered Tristan and Logan out the door. *Oh hell no! They could be thieves, or worse … serial killers.* She didn't know what Tristan was thinking, but she hoped his plan didn't include actually stepping into the RV with the strange, cheerful couple.

"You better have a plan, Tristan," she whispered when she managed to shake off chatty Kathy's grip.

"I do," he said, flashing her a smile, "but I doubt you're going to like it."

When chatty Kathy winked at her, Logan plastered a forced smile on her face. She may be born and bred in the East Coast, but she didn't do vehicles without heat. She didn't do RV's. And she definitely didn't do sharing small spaces with irresistible men and a talkative couple determined to learn their entire life story before the morning.

Lord, help me.

CHAPTER 5

"Now that we are safely in the car, I hope you know that I'm not speaking to you the rest of the drive to California," Logan said as she zipped her coat back up despite the fact that he had the heat in the SUV on full blast. He didn't care that they were taking side roads to avoid the cops. Adding an extra hour to their trip was a small price to pay.

"I warned you that you wouldn't like it, but at least we got out of that situation, right?"

"Yeah, but you let chatty Kathy feel me up like I was some cheap ass piece of meat."

Tristan laughed aloud although he knew it was only making the situation worse. "I had no choice. Chatty Kathy was at least semi-attractive. There was no way in hell I was letting two-teethed Ed touch any part of my body."

"Whatever," she grumbled as she crossed her arms over her chest. "How did you know they were swingers anyway?"

Tristan knew she was going to ask him that, but he didn't really want to share the whole truth with her. The minute they had walked into the lobby of the inn and been told there were no more rooms left, he'd been on high alert.

A quick survey of the lot showed about six other cars of people present, but there appeared to be at least twenty rooms total. When the guy at the front desk had done a quick flick of his head, Tristan had seen the couple slip through a side door. It had only taken a few seconds to figure out what type of stuff the couple was into.

"I noticed the way they were looking at us," he finally answered. "They probably pay the guy at the front desk to be their eyes and keep quiet while they are on the prowl. In small towns like this, I'd even bet that maybe that cop was involved, too."

"That's disturbing on so many levels. But I still don't see why *I* had to be the guinea pig."

"You had your shirt on the entire time."

"That doesn't make it any less creepy."

"Ed may appear to be running the show, but it's Kathy who holds the king card. The entire time she spoke to you, she was staring at your lips intently. It was freezing and snowing outside, but once she felt your breasts and I convinced them to start removing their clothes, I knew we had to make a run for it while their pants were around their ankles. The fact that neither of us had to remove anything other than our jackets proves how horny they were to get down to business."

"Eww, talking about them is making me nauseous," Logan muttered, shaking her head. "I will probably never look at anyone named Kathy or Catherine the same way again. I didn't notice any of that. I just thought they were strange as hell. I'm surprised swingers are even residing in a place that was so scarce of people."

"There is a swinger's club about five or so miles down the road. They weren't the most attractive, so they probably use

44

it to their advantage to catch other swingers when they hit the exit."

Belatedly, Tristan caught his mishap in mentioning the swinger's club. "I meant, I heard that there was a club nearby."

"Too late," she said, curling one leg under the other in her seat. "You've been to that swinger's club before, haven't you?"

Just lie, he thought to himself. The problem with lying is that he had done it so much when he discussed his past relationship that he was sick and tired of it.

"We just exited Wyoming and entered Utah. The Salt Lake City airport is a couple of hours away."

She looked at him inquisitively when he didn't respond to her question. "So does that mean yes, you have been to a swinger's club before?"

He stared straight ahead to the snowy highway and took a deep breath. There were only an extremely small number of people who knew about his ex, and confiding in a person he had met only twenty-four hours ago did not seem like the smartest idea. Especially if he had plans to bring down her company.

"My fiancée was into some kinky shit," he said with a forced laugh. He didn't glance over at her, but when she spoke he heard the catch in her voice.

"Oh, you're engaged," she said barely above a whisper. Had it not been so silent in the car, he may have missed it.

"Was engaged," he corrected. "She passed away four years ago." Only then did he finally steal a glance in Logan's direction. The look of sympathy in her eyes was precisely why he never told women about his deceased fiancée.

"I'm so sorry to hear that," she said, lightly placing her hand on his arm that was tightly gripping the steering wheel. He wished his coat hadn't concealed the warmth he knew he would get from her touch. Talking about his past still made him feel anxious at times.

"How did she pass away?"

"She developed a rare, non-contagious disease that attacked her immune system," he stated. "We found out a couple months into our engagement." Tristan left out the part where the day she received the news was the same day he was going to break off the engagement. Unfortunately, fear of the guilt he would feel afterward forced him to continue on with the engagement.

"That's heartbreaking." Logan scooted closer to him, as far as the seatbelt would let her. "So you were never able to get married?"

Although he hated the looks of sympathy he sometimes got from people who knew his story, the fact that Logan's voice slightly cracked when she spoke actually warmed his heart a bit.

"We never married, and six months after she received the news, she lost her battle to the disease." Tristan briefly took his eyes off the road to observe a silent Logan. She wasn't looking at him anymore, but instead, was facing the road absorbing everything he had told her.

"That's pretty awesome of you," she said sweetly. "Not many men would stick by a woman's side like that. Some, but not many."

There was a sadness in her voice that caught him off guard. A sadness that appeared deeper than what she was saying on the surface.

"I'd like to think most men would do exactly what I did," he replied. "But you disagree?"

In his peripheral view, he noticed her lightly rubbing the palm of her hands up and down her jeans. Apparently, he wasn't the only person getting anxious at the direction of their conversation.

"I guess since you shared a bit about yourself, I can share a bit about myself." He heard her words, but it sounded like she was talking more to herself than him.

"Long story short, my dad was involved in some illegal activity and tarnished my family's name. While I was attending Yale, I fell for a guy who I thought understood what I'd been through and accepted me for me. He was three years older than me, and he proposed my junior year. I said yes, and we were married right after I graduated. However, three months into our marriage, he told me he wanted a divorce."

Brains and beauty ... He'd already assumed as much when he had looked her up online, but after getting to know her a little, he was even more intrigued and wanted to know more.

"All of a sudden he wanted a divorce?"

"Sure did," she said firmly. "I worked two jobs while I was attending Yale, and even though he came from a well off family, his parents had cut him off when he decided not to go into the family business. I would give him money to help jump start his many business ventures, but his parents eventually decided to give him an ultimatum. He could get access to his trust fund again, *if* he divorced me. Apparently, they couldn't be associated with a criminal."

"Damn," Tristan said aloud, surprised at how much they had in common. "So basically your ex-husband was a coward and you had to pay for your father's mistakes? That's such bullshit."

He'd stayed with his ex because he'd known she didn't have anyone else, and a part of him hoped that she would grow to love him for him, and not his money. Back then, it was hard to see that the wannabe singer was only dating him for his connections to the industry through his customized watch business and Tristan had been too much in love to see through her bullshit.

"Pretty much," Logan agreed. "I guess it didn't matter that I was clearly on the path to solidifying a great career for myself, or that I'd graduated in the top ten percent of my class. Not meeting the social standards of their well-off family meant I had to go because staying with their son tarnished their image. And when asked to make the choice between money and me, my ex chose money ... every time. I don't completely blame him, though, because I shouldn't have been so naïve."

"Ah." He tried to calm his irritation, and finally began piecing together a few pieces of her puzzle. "So I'm guessing that's the reason why you founded High Class Society."

"It was definitely a deciding factor for me, but my friends and fellow founders each had their own reasons for wanting to create High Class Society. What you couldn't possibly understand from the screen shots you saw, is the fact that we give women the tools and encouragement to go after the man of their dreams ... despite the fact that they may not be in the same social class as the person they are pursuing."

"Like a matchmaking service," he interjected.

"Not like your typical matchmaking service," Logan replied. "Our female members build more of a sisterhood by sharing their stories about past relationships and encouraging one another in love and life in general. I guess if you combined a sorority and a matchmaking company, you would get a version of our organization, but we're still unique in our own way."

The passion in her voice was hard to miss, and Tristan hated to admit that her explanation actually painted High Class Society in a different light than he had originally thought. Nonetheless, he still despised what they stood for. At the end of the day, he was sure that at least a few members were just a bunch of leeching groupies disguising themselves as women of substance, and *that* was precisely the reason he couldn't let go of his mission to expose HCS and save the lives of some men who may fall victim to their undercover tactics.

"Enough about me," she said, adjusting in her seat. "Let's get back to you and your ex being into kinky stuff."

He laughed before responding. "Let's just say that while we were dating, I didn't always share her enthusiasm for trying something different, but if she was willing, I was willing." There were a few good times he had shared with his ex. It was just hard to remember them sometimes since the bad outweighed the good.

"So you watched her have threesomes? And that didn't excite you?"

"Not really," he said honestly. "I learned I don't like to share, and that was her thing, not mine. Even though it was sexy when she interacted with the women, I walked out when she was with the men. I was just there to make sure nothing happened to her."

Her silence spoke volumes, and he was sure he didn't seem like a man who loved his fiancée, but rather one who hadn't cared who she slept with. Or maybe she thought he was just doing what his dying love wanted.

"Well, I guess every couple has their secrets," she stated.

"I guess."

"Have you ... umm. Did you ..." Logan stumbled over her words a bit. "Have you dated anyone else seriously since she passed?"

"I didn't start dating until two years after she passed." *Mainly because it's hard to find a woman who doesn't want something from me ...* "There was this one woman who I connected with on a deeper level, but it didn't last."

He still thought about that woman every now and then, but being around Logan made him feel alive again. He may want to dislike her and what she stands for, but there was no denying the natural chemistry between them. He'd missed the feeling of lusting after a woman, so when this was all over and they found Sophia, at least he could thank Logan for that.

"I'm not dating anyone now if you're interested."

"I'm not," she answered quickly, causing him to laugh.

"Whatever you say sweetness," he replied. "How do you feel about stopping in Salt Lake for a night for something to eat, and getting back started in the morning? I'm a little tired and the weather is still pretty bad." Traveling down memory lane was suddenly not making him want to do anything other than sleep.

"Sounds like a plan."

CHAPTER 6

"*A*re you sure you're okay with the arrangement?" Tristan asked Logan for the third time. "I'll sleep on the sofa sleeper."

"It's fine," Logan replied as she opened her suitcase and pulled out what he assumed was pajamas. She had been antsy ever since two prior hotels told them that there weren't any vacancies. Although he was originally glad that they were able to get the last two rooms in the current hotel, when he'd noticed his room was extremely cold, he checked the thermostat and realized the nob was broken. After being told that it couldn't be fixed that night, he'd had no choice but to cancel the room and bunk up with Logan or freeze to death.

To be honest, he wasn't that happy about the arrangements, either; the main reason being that he wasn't sure if he could resist keeping his hands to himself while sharing a room with her. Of course he would be a gentleman and wouldn't make a move without being one hundred percent sure she wanted it, too. However, he wasn't looking forward to a possible night of blue balls.

What the fuck is wrong with me? It had been months since

he had even taken a real interest in a woman, and here he was acting like he was going on a first date rather a road trip to find his sister.

Sophia. He hadn't checked his tracking app for her in a while since he had been too busy trying to avoid the swingers and get them safely to a hotel for the night and out of the snowstorm.

"It looks like they had to stop, too," he said to Logan, who was still shuffling through her suitcase. "They are about four or five hours ahead of us, so we made pretty good time. We'll leave even earlier in the morning than I originally said if you're okay with that."

"That's fine." When she'd spoken, she had never even looked in his direction. *What is wrong with her?* Guaranteed, they didn't know a lot about each other, but he could sense her irritation and dismissal. For some reason, he couldn't let it go. He wanted to know what was bothering her, especially if he had something to do with it.

"Is there something you want to talk about?" he asked as he walked over to the bed and sat down next to her luggage. "You seem aggravated."

Her eyes rose from her suitcase and she gave him an examining look. He didn't know what she was searching for so he just stayed still and let her do the searching.

"Can I ask you another question?"

He wanted to say no, but found himself saying yes instead.

"Were you happy when you were engaged?" she asked, sitting next to him on the bed.

"That was random," he said with a laugh.

"I'm being serious."

He studied her expression and tried his best to ignore the enticing way she smelled. "At times, I suppose," he said dishonestly as he focused on a spot on the floor ... anything to avoid her eyes and possibly give away the truth. Tristan had spent a better part of the past few years trying to pretend like the actions of his ex hadn't fazed him, when in actuality, they had.

"I don't believe you," she said, calling out his lie. "You twitched slightly when you responded." He looked up from the floor to glance at her.

"You're intrigued because I'm right, aren't I?" she continued. "You weren't happy when you were engaged."

Who was this woman? And why was she able to read him better than most? Just as she had on the plane, she'd picked up on his actions. His sister often told him he twitched whenever he lied about his relationship.

"Like every couple, we had our ups and downs."

"But there were more downs than ups ... weren't there?"

He wanted to say something sarcastic, but he suspected she wouldn't back down from her questions. Quite frankly, he was glad she was finally back to talking to him anyway.

"Yes," he said truthfully. "There were more downs than ups. But we made it work."

"Because you loved her or because you knew her time on earth was limited?"

He returned his focus to the spot on the floor as he thought about the best way to respond to her question. He'd often thought about the real reason he had stayed with her, and after years of trying to figure out how he had been so gullible in the first place, he realized that he'd wanted to make his relationship work because he'd longed to have a loving relationship. He was never much for dating around and had always been more interested in building a foundation to start a family.

"I did love her," he admitted. "Unlike me, she didn't really have anyone growing up. So when we met, I felt like I had to be her everything."

"As I said earlier in the car ... that's pretty amazing of you."

"I'm not that great," he responded. "When my parents divorced and I saw what it did to my sister, I promised that when I had kids, I'd make sure my future children wouldn't have to go through that. When we started dating, I saw the possibility for a family and loving relationship."

"There's nothing wrong with believing in love."

He gave a slight chuckle. "I never said I didn't believe in love. I told you I truly did love her." He finally looked up from the floor again to glance at her, calculating his next words. "Unfortunately, my love wasn't enough for her. Since she cheated on me, her actions weren't that of a woman in love. And when she passed, I questioned if she ever really loved me at all."

He wondered if Logan knew how fast his heart was pumping whenever she looked at him like that. Like she could see things inside of him that others had failed to realize.

"I don't see how any woman could ever cheat on you." Honest eyes held his. The sincerity in her voice was undeniable.

"I appreciate that," he said, confirming her original assumption. "Just like your past relationship impacted your views, so did mine."

Logan winkled her nose. "I think the factor to remember in both of our experiences is that we can move forward from what happened. A failed relationship is not worth giving up on love. I tell my HCS ladies that every day, and I would be a liar if I didn't believe in what I preached. I know you're upset about Sophia running off with Justice Covington, and trust me, I grew really fond of your sister, so her disappearance has upset me, too. But did you ever stop and think that they are trying to do exactly what both of us have failed to do so far?"

"Which is finding the love of their life?"

"Exactly." Curling one foot under the other on the bed, Logan placed her hand on his arm. Unlike in the car, he felt her warmth this time.

"I don't doubt that Sophia and Justice care for one another, but he's eight years older than her and she hasn't lived enough life to know how tough relationships can be." He knew his sister was in love, but he wasn't sure exactly what Justice wanted with Sophia, and that fact made him uneasy since they were heading to Napa Valley, California.

"Just because she doesn't have enough experience, doesn't mean it isn't the real thing. Besides, I can't imagine why a twenty-four-year-old woman wouldn't open up to her thirty-four-year-old, overprotective brother," Logan said with sarcasm.

"I take offense to that," he replied, placing both hands over his heart. "I'll have you know that Sophia and I have a very close relationship."

"I don't doubt that," she said with a laugh. "I have younger sisters, too. Trust me, as close as we are, they don't tell me everything."

"Something tells me you're very intuitive, so they probably don't have to say much for you to pick up on their thoughts."

"I've always been able to read women well, but men are a different story. It seems like I'm always picking the wrong guy for me."

"I don't know about that," he responded as he observed the fact that they seemed to slowly be inching closer to one another. "You barely know me, but I'd say you've been reading me pretty well."

"You think so?" she asked a little breathlessly.

"You better not let it go to your head," he whispered, inching closer to her. When he'd first realized they were sharing a hotel room, he had agreed not to make a move unless he noticed signs that she was just as interested as he was. The rise and fall of her chest had increased its pace, and the sexual tension that filled the air was hot enough to melt the snow that was rapidly falling outside.

However, it was the look reflected in her eyes that was getting to him. The woman had a pair of bedroom eyes that he could only recall seeing once in his lifetime, and yet he was sure that Logan's were even more enticing. They had already been flirting since they met, but he was sure that even if she had decided to be mute during their entire road trip, her eyes would give away her attraction.

"Your eyes are strikingly beautiful," he said as he bounced from her eyes to her lips, then back to her eyes. "And intoxicating."

"Thank you." Her soft, breathless voice was turning him on even more. "I didn't think I'd ever hear you give me a compliment after some of the things you said when you stormed into my office."

He knew he'd said some harsh things, but upon discovering that his sister was missing, he had been reacting off emotion, which was so different than the way he usually conducted himself.

"I apologize for being rude. I'm usually not like that at all, but meeting you in person caught me off guard." He didn't want to elaborate, and the side smile that crossed her lips proved she understood exactly how he had felt.

"I know the feeling," she replied. "Guess there's always more to a person than what meets the eye." Her gaze dropped to his lips. When she licked her own, he couldn't take it anymore.

"I guess so," he said as he finally did the one thing he had been dying to do since they met. The minute his lips brushed against hers, he didn't have the patience to be sweet and gentle. His lips were hungry and precise, and the passionate way she was kissing him back caused him to increase the pressure.

When she lightly moaned and placed her hand on the back of his neck, it took all of his strength to keep his hands on her hips and not roam her body. The kiss went from hot to heavy in a matter of seconds, giving him a delectable idea of just how appetizing Logan Sapphire really was.

"Oh my," she said, breaking the kiss against Tristan's wishes. "I haven't had a kiss like that in a while."

"Me neither," he replied truthfully. "Since we're in agreement …" He let his voice trail off as he joined them together in another alluring kiss. Her thigh grazed his, and before he knew it, he was dragging them both further up on the bed.

He placed Logan securely on top of him in the cove of his legs—thighs to thighs, chests to chests, and hands on ass—and he was enjoying every succulent moment of their caressing kiss.

When she stopped for a second time and gazed down at him, he didn't hold back how horny he was. He wanted her to see it … wanted her to bear witness to the scorching hot lust that was flowing through his veins.

"It seems like I've known you for much longer than a day," she murmured.

"I know the feeling," he said in agreement. He wanted nothing more than to continue what they were doing, but Logan's lustful eyes were replaced by panic, and she scatted off the bed.

Suddenly, she grabbed her room key off the nightstand. "I need to take a walk."

"Um, now?" he asked, looking down at his pants. "I won't push you to do anything, but—"

"I know you won't," she quickly replied, cutting him off. "I'll be right back." With that, she was out of the door in two seconds flat.

"What in the hell was that about?" he said aloud as he dragged his fingers down his face. He hadn't read the situation wrong; Logan had definitely been as interested as he was. Although he wished he could blow off his irritation at her rejection and eagerness to escape him, a part of him— that vulnerable part that he rarely let show but had been revealing ever since he'd met Logan—was creeping to the surface of his mind.

"Great job, Derrington ... blue balls it is," he muttered to himself, yanking off his T-shirt in hopes that his body temperature would eventually return to normal.

CHAPTER 7

"**O**h my God, I think I might pass out."

"Calm down," the voice on the other line instructed. "What happened?"

"Jade, I think I'm in a little more trouble than I thought."

Jade Simone Daniels was a relationship therapist, as well as one of Logan's best friends and confidants. With the exception of her partners, Jade knew the most about her.

"Start from the beginning." As Logan paced the lobby, she explained to Jade the course of events over the past day.

"Okay," Jade said calmly. "So now you're in the hotel. You've told him a little more about the organization, which is good because it may help him realize what HCS is about. You both shared things about your life and he passionately kissed you. You said he's fine as hell, right?"

"Girl, *yes*," she hissed.

"Then why the heck are you on the phone with me?"

"Because that's not all." Logan was finally able to take a seat in a nearby chair. "I've felt connected with him from the start and I couldn't explain why. However, after hearing a bit more of his story and noticing this certain look about him when he starts to get sexually aroused, I think I may know him. He called me sweetness, and it wasn't the word itself, but rather the way he said it. I've heard that tone of voice before. Seductive ... hypnotizing. And the way he described my eyes. Oh God, it is him." She closed her eyes tightly before opening them again.

"Um, okay ... now I'm confused. You aren't sure if you know him or not?"

"Exactly!"

"Wait, how the hell is that possible?"

"I've never personally met him, but if my suspicions are right, we are very well acquainted with each other physically."

"How is that ... oh no," Jade said, finally catching on. "Please tell me you're joking."

"I wish I was."

"You can't tell him the truth, Lo, you know that."

"Yeah, I understand. But I'm freaking out over here!"

"What did you say his name was again?"

"I didn't," Logan replied, "but it's Tristan Derrington."

"Oh shit. I must admit, I think you may be right. I've seen his name before. Do you want me to check our contracts?"

"Ugh, I was afraid you were going to say that. Yeah, check for me please."

"Okay, but this could be a good thing," Jade replied. "If you're right, he is already bound in contract."

"Not for HCS. Besides, what am I supposed to say to him?"

"I know I said don't tell him the truth, but maybe the truth would work."

"Hmm, I can visualize that convo now," she replied sarcastically. "So, Tristan, remember how you found out about HCS, a secret organization I founded? Well, I'm also a member of another secret female organization founded by my best friend, Jade. And in that organization, most of the members spend every Friday living out our wildest sexual fantasies with men who sign a contract to agree to be our secret weekly fuck buddy. I've only been with one man through that organization though because I started to catch feelings and build an emotional attachment, which is totally against the rules. Oh, and by the way, since we require members and the men to wear body paint, sexy costumes or half masks to conceal all of our identities, I can't confirm that you and I were having sex for over six months, but I'm pretty sure your dick knows my vagina very well."

The line went silent for a few seconds. "Umm ... maybe you want to leave out the part about me being the founder," Jade replied. "No use bringing us both down."

"Seriously," Logan dropped her head into her hands, "that's all you have to say?"

"Lo, do you remember why you decided to no longer participate in the Friday sexcapades?"

"Of course."

"His code name for Friday night was Hunter, right? That's what he asked you to call him?"

"Yes, and my undercover name was Blue. I always spoke to him in my British accent and he spoke with a French accent. It was like our thing."

"Exactly. After you stopped coming, we received a written letter from Hunter stating that if Blue wasn't participating anymore, neither was he."

Her head flew up from her hands. "You never told me that. Here I was thinking another member had snatched him up."

"That's because you were already in too deep with your feelings for him, and I knew meeting each other in real life was against the rules. You're my girl, but I couldn't jeopardize the organization."

"You know I understand. Bending the rules jeopardizes everything."

"That's true." Jade added, "But maybe this is a sign that rules or not, you can't tempt fate. If he walked back into your life, that means something. So maybe you should find out once and for all if the feelings you felt in the heat of those Friday nights can be translated into something more meaningful."

Sighing, Logan slumped in her chair. "And how do you suppose I do that?"

"Well, you both are already getting to know each other, and since you only have this road trip, you have to make the most of it. Since you met in the bedroom, maybe see if your bodies remember each other sexually."

"Why? To see if Tristan really is Hunter like I think he is?"

"Oh no, girl," Jade said with a laugh. "I already looked through our online contracts. Tristan and Hunter are the same person, so you were right on the nose with that assumption. I simply suggested having sex with him because you've been a little bitchy ever since you stopped."

"And on that note, I'm ending this call."

"That's fine …as long as your sexual drought ends tonight, too. Good luck, boo!"

After she'd hung up the phone, Logan rolled her neck in a circle to try and ease the tension. Being around Tristan already made her nervous as hell, and now she was supposed to initiate sex with him?

"How in the world can I do that without bringing up feelings I thought I'd buried?" she asked herself aloud. She couldn't foresee how this situation would end, but she knew Jade was right. It was time to see if her body remembered Tristan as much as her mind did. Usually, she would make a man work harder to have sex with her, but considering they had already unknowingly been intimate, she was convinced it was time to make an exception.

* * *

WHEN SHE ARRIVED BACK to the room and slid her key card through the slot, she immediately stopped in the doorway at the sight of him lying on the bed. He had one arm draped over his eyes while the other was placed across his naked stomach. A quick glance at her cell showed she'd been gone for at least thirty minutes, and his even breathing proved that he'd drifted off to sleep.

Out of the corner of her eye, she saw her pajamas draped across the chair with her cosmetics bag sitting on the nearby coffee table. She quietly picked up both items and made her way to the bathroom to freshen up and change.

"Yes," she whispered when she noticed the standing shower with the large showerhead at top, and two smaller showerheads underneath to ensure water directly pounded every part of the body. She needed a hot shower after the realization that she had unknowingly agreed to go on a road trip with the one man she hadn't been able to get out of her mind. She discarded her clothes and tied up her hair before stepping in the shower.

As the water rushed over her body, she thought about the last sexual tryst she'd had with Hunter, or Tristan ... whatever the name, it didn't matter. For at least two or three Fridays a month for six months, Blue and Hunter had explored each other's bodies and ignored all caution that they were developing something deeper than a weekly romp in the sheets. But that last night they'd had sex, she'd decided that she couldn't continue seeing him. They had already broken so many rules by sharing certain things about themselves and the past relationships that had led them to one another. She had felt like she was in too deep, and since revealing their true identities was against the rules, she'd known that telling him the truth would jeopardize everything.

She closed her eyes as a few drops of water bounced off her body and hit her face. Her lathered loofah was soon forgotten as her thoughts continued to take precedence over everything else. She thought back to the conversations they'd had when they were body painting one another in the dim lighting of the room they'd chosen for one of their Friday sexual rendezvous.

"Oh wow," she murmured, suddenly remembering a few key things he'd shared with her months ago. From talking to Tristan a couple of hours ago, she knew that he hadn't really been happy when he was engaged, but he never expanded on the subject matter. Remembering what Tristan had told her when he was concealed as Hunter, pieced together the remainder of his story.

"She wasn't just a cheater. His ex had only been interested in him for his money," she said quietly to herself. Hunter had never told her, or better yet told Blue, the reason why he had felt obligated to stay with his ex, nor had he told her why they weren't together any longer. Now she knew why ... he'd felt obligated. She had been sick, and even though she'd cheated on him—with more than one man according to Hunter—he'd known she didn't have anyone and he couldn't let her die alone.

The realization that he'd placed his bitterness aside to be there for his fiancée only heightened emotions that she'd spent the last few months trying to ignore. When she'd been acting as Blue, she had told him that her ex-husband had asked for a divorce and broken her heart, but she hadn't expanded on the reasoning behind it, just how she'd felt as a result of a failed marriage.

He'd been there for her and had offered her comfort that she hadn't felt in a long time. By the end of her shower, she was absolutely positive about one thing: she'd fallen for Hunter when she hadn't even known much about the man behind the mask. Now, after knowing a little bit more about him, she was falling for Tristan, the man who was determined to expose HCS and everything she'd worked hard to keep a secret.

Even with the ultimatum of exposing what she knew or keeping those facts to herself staring her in the face, she couldn't pass up the opportunity to be with him again. A part of it felt wrong since he had no clue that she was Blue—his Blue—but she needed him and *longed* for him to be inside of her.

She put on her tank top and shorts before placing a few dabs of her favorite perfume in the areas she hoped would reel him in. She had almost not brought the perfume with her on the trip because she hadn't worn it since she was with Hunter. Now she was glad she had it with her, and hoped he would react to the scent in the same predatory way he had in the past.

She tiptoed into the bedroom, satisfied to find him still asleep. She wasn't sure if falling asleep without a shirt was done by accident or if he'd had every intention on torturing her with scored abs. Walking over to his sleeping body, she licked her lips. She couldn't resist gliding her fingers across the curves of his body. Rough in some parts, smooth in others … just like she remembered. *They look even better up close and not concealed by body paint.*

He stirred in his sleep, evidence that her fingers were eliciting a reaction. If she were bold enough to cup him though his pants, she would. However, it seemed too forward, so instead, she lifted herself onto the bed and straddled him. When she rotated her hips in slow, small circles, she watched his chest heave a little faster than before as his body stirred awake.

He removed the arm that was covering his face, but his eyes still remained closed. Despite the fact that he hadn't opened his eyes, his hands went to grip her butt, steadying her on the part he wanted her to continue to ride. She increased the twirl of her hips and continued to run her fingers up and down his abs.

She couldn't wait anymore; she had to run her lips across his body. The last time they had kissed, she had been caught off guard with the emotions he had provoked within her. Now, she was ready for those passionate feelings to resurface.

With the slyness of a grey fox, she slowly bent her torso bringing her lips closer to his. She anticipated nervousness to be written across her face, so she appreciated the fact that his eyes remained closed.

When she was a couple of inches away, she hesitated. She had always been a decisive person, but right now, she was second-guessing herself. *What if having sex isn't the right answer? What if I'm supposed to just be satisfied with the memory of Hunter and the fact that he now has a real identity?* After all, secret identities were secret for a reason. *What if the time we spent together on those Friday nights were all we were supposed to share together?*

Her thoughts were bouncing back and forth like a Ping-Pong ball. *What if this is my chance at true love?* What if every experience she had with the opposite sex was to prepare her for this moment with Tristan?

Mind finally made up, she ventured the last couple of inches toward his lips. When she was so close she could almost taste him, his eyes flew open, capturing hers in a way that made her breath catch in her throat. *Lord have mercy.* Had he not chosen to wrap his arms around her in that moment, she surely would have jumped back at the intensity in his eyes. He wanted her. Badly. And the want and need reflected in his eyes was extremely dangerous. Dangerous for her body and for her mind ... but especially dangerous for her heart.

When he lifted his head and seized her lips in a greedy kiss, she had no choice but to return his mind-blowing kiss lick by lick.

CHAPTER 8

*T*ristan wasn't sure what had changed her mind, but when his body had awakened to a sweet pair of honey thighs straddling him, it had taken all of his energy to let Logan remain in control.

Now that his lips were devouring hers, he couldn't control the sexual urge he'd been trying to keep at bay since they'd met. Usually, it took him a while to set his sights on a woman he wanted to be intimate with. He wasn't really into having multiple sex partners and preferred one woman at a time. He hadn't purposely chosen to be celibate the past couple of months, but after having sex with a couple women in an effort to try and forget about a woman who often maintained most of his thoughts, he had decided that it was best if he just focus on his work.

As most men usually do, he thought about sex all of the time, but Logan was the first woman in months that made him actually *crave* sex. There was something about her that had intrigued him from the start. Now, feeling her return his kisses with the same fervor he felt, was almost too much to handle.

Lifting her with ease, he switched their positions so that he was on top and she was planted securely underneath him. He began kissing her collarbone, easing the straps of her tank top off as he did so. A few more tugs of her shirt, and her breasts popped free of the material.

"Beautiful," he said softly as he latched on to one brown nipple pulled it into his mouth. Her breasts fit perfectly in the palm of his hand, and the sounds of her moans caused him to increase the flicks of his tongue making sure to give both breasts an equal amount of attention.

He eased her tank top over her head, giving him better access while his hands roamed to her shorts and slipped inside. He stopped suckling her breasts long enough to give her a surprised glance at the fact that she wasn't wearing any panties beneath her shorts. He discarded the material on the floor to join her top, leaving her completely naked and sprawled out on the bed.

Just like I thought. She was even more beautiful without a stitch of clothing. He wasted no time spreading her pussy lips apart and dipping his finger in her center, satisfied to find her already wet. His thumb twirled around her clit, matching the movement of his finger that was already stroking her insides.

As much as he wanted to submerge himself inside of her, he wanted to taste her even more. Her moans began growing more rapid, urging him to replace his fingers with his mouth. Without warning, he slid down and lifted her hips off the bed while bringing her center to his mouth. Sweet sobs vibrated throughout her body and echoed in his ears that were covered by the insides of her thighs.

When she gripped his head and held him in place, he dived deeper, rotating his tongue even faster than before. After he'd first walked into her office and taken a thorough glance at her, he'd thought she'd looked as delectable as strawberries and champagne … sweet, yet classy … juicy, yet smooth. Now that he'd gotten a chance to taste the purpose of his fixation, he confirmed that she tasted just like he had thought she would.

Her pants let him know she was close. A few flicks of his tongue over her lips and a couple more sucks of her clit, and she released an orgasm that rocked her entire body. She squirmed in his hands, but he refused to let her go. He kept her planted firmly on his mouth until he was certain she had released every last drop.

"Oh my God," she said breathlessly. "That was …" Her voice trailed off, but he didn't mind that she couldn't formulate any words. He could barely form a complete sentence in his mind, so he refused to try and say anything out loud.

She perused his body. "I can't be the only one naked," she murmured as her hands went to the button on his jeans and made quick work with the zipper.

"We can't have that now, can we," he agreed as he briefly hopped off the bed to remove the rest of his clothes. He'd planned to get right back in bed after he was finished undressing, but the seductive way Logan was admiring his physique kept his feet planted.

He was already aroused, but the thirst in her eyes made his erection grow even more.

"Fascinating," she exhaled, crooking her finger for him to come closer. His walk may have looked suave and smooth, but internally, he felt like he could come just from the way she was looking at him. His need for her was that strong.

After he protected them both, he rejoined her on the bed and removed the clip from her hair so that he could run his fingers through her tresses. She leaned her head back into his hand and let out another soft moan as he caressed her head. His lips sought out hers for another seductive kiss just as his erection found her center.

Glancing down at her for confirmation, he was gratified when she nodded her head in agreement. Needing no other assurance, he slid through her plush, soft lips and entered her in one smooth thrust.

They both shared a groan of satisfaction when he was embedded deep inside of her core. When her legs wrapped around his waist, he lifted himself in somewhat of a squat to try and hit her sweet spot and bring him even deeper inside. He knew he'd succeeded when her moans turned into a catlike purr as she met him thrust for thrust.

Moving inside of her felt better than perfect. It felt like he was coming … *home.* Instantly his eyes flew to hers, a little taken aback by the feelings reflected in them. Her eyes had been closed since he'd intimately connected them, but now her thoughts were written all over her face. What he was seeing wasn't just lust and passion, it was something more … something deeper.

What the hell is going on? Why did it feel like they had done this erotic dance before? It was as if their bodies knew this sweet seduction better than their minds did. Unexpectedly, she closed her eyes and threw her head back. Tristan didn't know if it was because she was on the brink of another orgasm or if she was shutting him out from the feelings evident in her eyes.

As he felt his body tense with each move and grow harder by the second, he didn't have time to reflect on her reasoning. All he could do was release the powerful orgasm that matched the potency of the orgasm Logan was releasing at the same time.

What is it with this woman? He wondered as he rode out the passionate convulsions. It wasn't the first time he had asked himself that question, and he was pretty sure that it wouldn't be the last.

71

* * *

It's him, she thought as he went to the bathroom and returned with a hot towel that he used to wipe her clean and soothe her core.

Although Jade had already confirmed that Tristan and Hunter, her mystery lover, were the same person, making love to him just solidified that fact even more. Oh man, she'd missed their unworldly connection and the fire he ignited within her.

When he got back in the bed, she turned her body around so that her butt was pressed up against him. Usually, a random hook up wouldn't include spooning of any kind. Yet despite the knowledge he lacked regarding their past relationship, all she could do was remember how safe she used to feel when he wrapped her up in his arms.

He took the bait and pulled her closer to him, the faint scent of his cologne teasing her nostrils in the most seductive way. She reminisced on the first time he had pulled her to him. It was after they had already had sex a few times, but the way he had held her felt different. It had felt special, and they had connected in a way neither of them had expected or been prepared for.

"Are you okay?" he asked. She had been silent, probably more silent than he preferred. *Was she okay?* She didn't quite know how to answer a question that seemed simple, but was loaded with meaning.

"In this exact moment, I'm perfect," she replied, looking back at him with a smile.

"Good," he said, teasing her with a tempting smile of his own. "Because I'm not done with you yet." She gasped when she felt him nudging her legs open as he slid into her with one smooth stroke.

"And now I'm perfect, too." Gripping her tightly, he

increased the speed of his pumps. Her moans grew louder and mingled with his groans, surely giving their neighbors a great idea of what was going down in their hotel room.

As much as she loved it sideways, she really wanted to feel his hands on her ass. Using what little strength she had, she lifted herself onto her knees, glad that he had followed her direction.

She wiggled her butt to get the perfect angle, and then wiggled it once more when he damn near howled out into the room. *He always did like this*. And what he'd liked even more was the way she was able to pop her butt as he thrust inside of her.

She angled her body once more to perform the move that used to make him lose all control.

"Holy shit," he bellowed, gripping her hips to try and keep up with her movements. With every pop and twist of her hips, he let out another howl until his words were almost incorrigible.

"I'm close," she moaned, trying to prolong her orgasm. She couldn't really make out his response, but she assumed he was letting her know that he was on the brink as well.

When his hips increased their motion in an almost desperate fashion, she clenched him even harder, determined to milk him dry of everything he had to offer. For her, this was more than sex or quenching a hunger they had for one another. It was reconnecting with the one man she was convinced would remain on her mind for the rest of her life.

As dismissive as she could be with the opposite sex, it was really quite sad that she already knew she couldn't be that way with Tristan. Dismissing him was not an option. Her body just wouldn't allow her to do that.

She pushed all of her thoughts to the side and allowed herself to enjoy their bodies coming together in one hot, satisfying moment.

While they lay on the bed, still intertwined in one another, she couldn't resist a glance at his face. When their eyes locked, her intake of breath faltered at the question she saw there.

He's trying to figure it out, she thought. *He's trying to figure out why having sex with me feels so familiar.* And damned if she didn't want to just come right out and tell him that she was his mystery woman. She was the one he'd called Blue ... the one he'd once said he'd connected with more than he had any other woman.

However, fear of his response and rejection kept her lips sealed tight. *Maybe we could start something new?* She shook her head in disagreement the minute the thought entered her mind. His eyes remained on hers, and it seemed he wasn't in the mood to talk any more than she was. Scooting close to him on the bed, she wrapped her arms around him in a tender hug.

He didn't push her away, but instead returned her hug and placed a sweet kiss on her forehead.

CHAPTER 9

*I*t was still cold outside, but soft, white flakes were starting to dwindle as they fell from the Utah sky, indicating that they were close to the Nevada border. Tristan had heard on the car radio that many smaller airplanes in Denver were still grounded, so he was still glad they had chosen to drive. They had gotten an early start, and now they were finally close to catching up with his sister.

"We made up lots of ground. We're only two hours apart now."

"That's great," Logan said, placing her hand over her stomach, "but if you don't feed me soon, I may have to take over the wheel."

On its own accord, his stomach growled right along with hers. "Maybe we do have time to grab a bite to eat."

"Finally, I get something I want," she teased, raising her hands in the air as much as the SUV would allow.

"Hmm, I'm pretty sure I was giving you everything you wanted last night," he faced her with a smirk on his face and a gleam in his eye, "and this morning."

She was already shaking her head at him. "You are way too arrogant. Last night was good, but it wasn't *all that.*"

His head whipped toward her so fast that the car moved with his body.

"Try not to get into an accident," she said with a laugh. "It's still snowing outside, and yesterday's snow has turned into ice."

"Are you telling me that last night wasn't great for you?" He didn't believe her. Not for one second. Her body had been craving his last night as much as his had been feigning for hers.

"It was good," she said with a shrug. He refused to look at her again for fear that he would jerk the car, but he could hear the laughter in her voice.

"Oh, look, there's a diner at the next exit. Can we stop there for food?"

"Sure," he replied, although their conversation about the course of events last night was far from over. He was a confident man—always had been and would probably always be self-assured—and last night had exceeded any expectations he had ever had about the opposite sex. His views may be slightly jaded, but despite his past failed relationship, he still believed in the ability to form an indescribable connection with someone. One that defied logic and snuck up on you when you least expected it.

Logan was that for him. She was that indescribable connection that he hadn't seen coming. Last night, he wasn't exactly sure why, had felt like a defining moment in his life. A moment that was new and intriguing, yet familiar at the same time. Like a new pair of shoes that was the same brand, style, and color as the old shoes you'd just worn to the sole.

He was still deep in thought when they parked the car, wrestled through the cold air swishing through their coats, and entered the restaurant.

"Are you okay?" she asked after they were seated and had ordered drinks and food.

"I'm fine," he said with a side smile.

"You've been quiet since we left the car."

"I'm good. Are you okay?"

She gave him a disbelieving look. "Perfect," she answered with an extra perk in her voice as she bit her lip and wiggled in her seat.

"What are you up to?" he asked, picking up on her sneakiness.

Instead of responding to him, she smiled a smile so sly, he was tempted to reach across the table and kiss her senseless, giving the ten or so other occupants in the restaurant a good show. Fortunately, she beat him to the foreplay.

"You're full of surprises," he said when he felt a foot slowly making its way up his leg. He didn't know how she'd removed her boot so quickly and damned if he even cared. When her foot reached his thigh, he squirmed in his seat and glanced around to see if anyone had caught on to what they were doing.

"Someone may see you," he grunted right before she reached the part of him she'd been searching for.

"You strike me as the type of man who isn't afraid to take risks."

He'd heard what she said, but it took him a minute to respond. "Finally, something we agree on."

"I guess your silence didn't mean you checked your arrogance at the front door of the restaurant."

"You didn't check your teasing at the door so why would I be lenient?"

"Well, if that's the case," she said with a shrug as she removed her foot.

"Wait, that's not what I meant." Reaching under the table for her foot, his pursuit quickly became a game of cat and mouse. They were still laughing and fooling around when the waitress returned to bring them the coffees they'd ordered.

He took out his smartphone and checked the tracking device for his sister. "It looks like they stopped, too," he stated after tapping his touchscreen. "They've been at the same location for the past twenty minutes."

"Even with all the snow, I'm sure we'll catch up to them with your driving."

As she took a sip of coffee, she gazed over her cup at him with those same bedroom eyes he'd really gotten used to seeing over the past couple days. Somehow, talking about his sister reminded him of the entire reason why they were together in the first place. He hated to admit it, but he wasn't ready for his time with Logan to end.

"Food's up, folks," the waitress said as she placed their plates of food on the table. While they dug into some much needed nourishment, they caught the attention of a young boy two tables over. When he waved, Tristan waved back with a smile.

A few minutes prior, he had noticed one of the waitresses paying close attention to the boy, and by the way he beamed up at her, he'd bet she was his mother.

"You like kids?" Logan asked when she followed his gaze.

"I've always liked kids," he replied after he'd taken a bite of his food. "What I wouldn't give to be young and carefree again. Do you like kids?"

"I love them," she replied with a smile. "I don't have any of my own, but I imagine that nothing is more rewarding than the love of a child or the unconditional love you give that child."

He gave her a somewhat forced smile, once again caught in his thoughts. "I definitely agree with you about that."

They continued to eat in silence, but he felt her eyes on him. Studying him … observing him.

"What's wrong?" he asked, noticing the concern written across her face before he looked down at his plate to continue eating.

"Your ex fiancée … she was pregnant, wasn't she?"

Tristan's eyes flew from his plate to Logan. "What makes you ask that?"

Her eyes softened. "Because back in the hotel when I said you were pretty amazing, you talked about wanting to provide a better life for your future children and not wanting them to go through what Sophia went through when your parents divorced. You took the conversation there, so I just assumed."

When he didn't speak, she continued. "And I also noticed how you were just watching that little boy who left the restaurant."

"Let's go back to the part when you said I was amazing," he smirked, trying to change the subject. Never, *ever*, had he met a woman as intuitive as Logan.

"Don't change the subject." She released a slight laugh before returning to the previous conversation. "You don't have to answer … I just want to make sure you're okay with whatever happened." She stumbled over her words a bit. "I don't mean to get in your business, I'm sorry."

"No need to apologize," he reassured, finally getting over the shock of her assumption. Truthfully, he'd been caught off guard because he had never told anyone why he'd really felt even more obligated to remain with his ex even after learning about her affairs and disease.

"She was pregnant when she got the news," he said, surprised at how much relief he felt finally getting the words out. "She'd been having dizzy spells before, but the day she got the tests results was the day she also received news of her pregnancy." Even now, he wasn't sure if he would ever forget that day. To this day, he wasn't even sure if the baby was his, but it hadn't mattered … he'd been prepared to step in and be a father.

"That must have been awful," she said, shuffling some food around her plate but not really eating anything. "To find out she's pregnant at the same time she found out she had a disease?"

He glanced back down at his plate. "In case you're wondering, she lost the baby at four months." It had been a while, but the loss still affected him.

"I'm so sorry you had to go through that," she whispered as she reached over and gently placed her hand on top of his.

"Thanks," he said, accepting her comfort, "but she went through a lot more than I did with the loss."

"And you stayed by her side the entire time," she reminded him. "Like I said before … you're amazing."

He searched her eyes, finding the sincerity of her words in them. "One day I hope to have a family, but I've also learned that everything happens for a reason. I can't dwell on the past … just grow from each experience."

A pleased smile crept on her face. "I agree. That's a good attitude to have."

"You better watch yourself, Ms. Sapphire," he teased, returning her smile. "You've been giving me more compliments than insults, so I do believe that means we're growing on each other."

"And just that quickly, the moment is gone," she replied with a laugh, as they both returned to eating.

* * *

"THERE'S one more thing left to settle before we get in the

car." Tristan rounded the corner to the passenger's side just as she'd opened the car door.

"Whatever it is can't wait until we get inside the car?" she asked as she shivered slightly when the wind picked up. The temperature had dropped a few degrees since they'd arrived at the restaurant and Logan was eager to warm up in the car.

"Nope." He stated the word with finality, causing her to take notice of his actions. He'd at least started the ignition, but somehow he'd conveniently placed his firm thigh in-between her legs and stopped her access into the vehicle.

"We have to clear up the matter about last night. You enjoyed yourself," he said, capturing her with penetrating brown eyes. He lingered over her lips until her breaths began to quicken before kissing the sweet spot behind her right ear.

"I'd felt it in the passionate way you returned my kisses last night …" he whispered in her ear. "I also felt it in the way your hands rubbed against my abs when you thought I was sleeping." He let his hands graze up and down her thighs, and even through her jeans she swore she felt his fingertips tease her skin.

"Your body's response to me was so potent, I knew only having you one time would never be enough. I wanted to be consumed by you … I still do."

She fidgeted under the warm breath teasing her neck. "Smooth talker. I bet you say that to all the women."

"I don't." Lifting his head, he looked back into her eyes, his desire confirming his words. "As a matter of fact, I don't think I've ever been this obsessed with a woman's taste before."

She moaned, unable to stop the sound from escaping her lips. She didn't know if it was the fact that he was using words like *consumed* or *obsessed*, but within seconds, her panties were drenched and her sexual urges heightened. He had barely touched her. Hadn't even kissed her. Yet, his words were flowing over her in the sweetest form of lovemaking.

When he finally kissed her, she let him control every part of the kiss, happy to lose control in his lethal mouth ... a mouth that had been doing such naughty things to her last night. The memory of it only aroused her more.

Just as her arms began to curl around his neck, he ducked and took a step back.

"Payback sucks doesn't it?" he asked with a smile as he walked to the driver's side of the car. "That will teach you to play with me in a restaurant and not finish what you started."

She stood there for a few seconds with her hands still in mid-air and stared out into the beautiful backdrop of mountains. She finally turned around to see his smug grin and hopped in the car before she gave him even more to laugh at.

"Just so you know," she said, buckling her seatbelt with a little more force than necessary, "I hate you."

CHAPTER 10

$\mathcal{L}$eaning out of the window, Logan let the warm wind brush over her face and lace through her hair.

"Fifty-five degrees beats twenty-five degrees any day in my book." She closed her eyes and soaked in the warmth, ignoring the large grey clouds waiting to be squeezed dry.

"Ah, the silent beauty finally decides to speak," Tristan said sarcastically.

She leaned back in the car and glared at him. "I was sleep for about three or four hours and I did speak to you a little despite the fact that I've decided I hate you," she explained with a mockingly quick smile.

They were leaving the San Francisco area and headed to Napa Valley. According to what Tristan had told her an hour prior, his sister had arrived to her destination, so time was of the essence.

She'd caught him looking at the digital clock quite a bit when he'd realized she had arrived in Napa, and even though she could see worry written in his facial features, he hadn't once voiced his concern out loud.

"How were you so sure your sister would be headed to Napa Valley?" she asked, realizing that he'd never elaborated on how he knew exactly where his sister and Justice were headed.

He glanced over at her before turning back to the narrow wine country road. "Remember when I told you how hard Sophia took our parents' divorce?"

"Of course."

"Well, I left out the fact that our parents didn't even officially get married until Sophia was six and I was sixteen, so we were in our parents' wedding."

"Wow, that's interesting. How long were they married?"

"Eleven years, which in my opinion was eleven years too long." He turned down another long and narrow road. "They had lived together, but had never been officially married. Sophia had always ignored the signs and believed that our parents were meant to be together. They are good people, but they never really grasped the whole parenting thing, so it was really just Sophia and I growing up. She never understood that they were actually better people apart than they ever were together."

"There are a lot of people who share the same hopes as Sophia."

"I know," he said in agreement, "but for Sophia, our parents being happy together was all she ever wanted for her birthday and Christmas gifts. I think it really broke my parents' heart to hear her gush about what perfect parents they were together when deep down, they knew it wasn't true."

"What about you?" she asked. "How did you feel?"

"To be honest," he briefly took his eyes off the road to look at her, "I never really understood how they got together in the first place. They never seemed to be a good match, but they had dated all through high school and college. From what I've been able to piece together from relatives, they were going to break up when my mom found out she was pregnant with me. They weren't the best example of a loving relationship, but they love us both in their own unique way, so that's all that matters to me."

"I feel the same way about my parents," Logan stated, nodding her head in agreement. "I have four sisters, and my mom tried to stay married to my dad for as long as she could when he began getting into trouble with the law. But eventually she had to move on, and we were happy when she did. Now she's remarried and happier than ever."

"That's great that she re-married. My mom and dad are both dating, but neither remarried ... at least not yet," Tristan said. "If you don't mind me asking, what about your dad?"

"Still in jail for all of his wrong doings, and that list is way too long to get into. Yet, despite his mistakes, he'll always be my dad."

Movement outside of her passenger window got her attention. Logan observed a busload of people piling out into a gravel parking lot of a quaint winery. Everything was so beautiful, she wished she could actually enjoy some time alone with Tristan at the wineries without being on a mission. She wanted to find Sophia, but she could also admit that she was a little disappointed that their trip was coming to an end.

Suddenly, she remembered that he still hadn't fully answered her question. "So why did your sister come to Napa?"

"Our parents were married in an elegant wine country estate," he answered. "And my sister always says the day my parents married was the happiest day of her life despite the fact that she was so young."

She watched his facial muscles tense and his hands clamp the steering wheel harder than necessary. "She always swore that the place our parents said their vows would be the place she would tie the knot."

She nodded her head, finally understanding why he'd been so sure Sophia was headed to California and not Las Vegas. "So now Sophia is trying to marry Justice in the same place your parents married," she said as a statement rather than a question. "I've personally never met Justice, but I've heard nothing but great things about him. How did they meet anyway?"

"I introduced them," he replied with a loud sigh lined with regret. "The summer right before Sophia's freshman year of college, she was avidly searching for an internship in her major, Computer Science. I'd met Justice through a mutual friend a few years prior and he'd just opened his start-up business, which you know is now one of the most successful social media platforms. He just so happened to have an internship opportunity, and without question, he glanced at Sophia's resume' and told me she had the internship."

He tensed even more as he talked. "Had I known he would fall in love with my teenage sister and prey on her weakness for romance, I would have said to hell with him and that internship."

Now it was clear why Tristan was so hell bent on finding his sister. He felt responsible for her relationship with Justice. "You make it seem like he took advantage of her," Logan replied. "I've never seen them together, so I can't really say. However, I have had the chance to get to know Sophia a little and from what I can tell, she's feistier than you give her credit for and goes after what she wants. If she decides or already has married Justice, I'm sure the decision was mutual."

"Maybe, but he's not innocent in this. They are eight years apart, and at her age, that's light years away."

"Not anymore," she rebutted. "I can see how that would have been an issue when she was eighteen, but you didn't see Sophia when we set up her profile. She was dead set on getting close to Justice no matter how hard we told her that would be. Justice is the founder of a huge social media network, yet he is rarely seen in the social scene and has been like that for the past couple years. He's never really been seen dating anyone and hasn't been spotted with any women. But the last two years, he rarely attended events and sent someone else from his staff on his behalf …" she said as her voice trailed off.

She studied Tristan's face, the hard lines of his jaw telling her that she was on to something. "It's because he proposed to Sophia and they couldn't be together … isn't it? That's why he stopped going to events?"

He remained silent as he looked over at her before turning back to the road. She wasn't sure if he was going to confirm or deny her assumption.

"Justice and I have a lot in common, so naturally we became friends after he gave Sophia that internship. Sophia and Justice had kept their relationship a secret from me," he finally stated. "I found out about them a couple months before he proposed and there was no way in hell I was letting my sister marry him."

"She didn't marry him because you didn't approve?"

"Every now and then at gatherings, I'd catch him watching my sister intently, so a few times I asked Justice if he was interested in her. He told me no each and every time. I understand having secrets, but when an opportunity presents itself to come clean, take the opportunity. He didn't do that. So yes, I don't think she married him because I didn't approve. We've always been extremely close. However, my parents didn't approve either."

"Don't you think you were being slightly unreasonable?

At least now I see why you figured they would definitely be getting married here in Napa."

"We've finally arrived, so we should find out soon enough," he said as they pulled into a gorgeous wine estate covered in green vines that appeared to stretch across the entire building.

As they exited the vehicle, she let his words linger for a while in her mind. She had to agree that one should come clean of secrets if the possibility presented itself to come clean. The last thing she wanted to do was tell Tristan that she was also Blue.

She'd even coincidently brought her gorgeous blue sapphire ring with her that represented her September birth month. It was the one object she'd constantly worn during their Friday fantasy nights.

"The time has come," she mumbled to herself. She would tell Tristan the truth before they left Napa. She wasn't sure if he would be receptive to the news. Hell, she wasn't even sure he still planned to out her company. Regardless, it was time for her to come clean ... even if she was scared to death that the one man who'd she'd opened up to unlike any other, may reject her. The one man she needed in her life.

"You've got to be fucking kidding me," she said a little louder than she intended.

"Why are you cursing?" he asked with a laugh as he held open the door of the estate's entrance.

"No reason." She ignored the inquisitive look he was giving her. Actually, her head was swarming with curse words she wished she could yell into the sky at the realization that she wasn't just afraid to get rejected by her former fuck buddy. She was afraid to get rejected by a man she'd fallen in love with.

CHAPTER 11

*T*ristan glanced around the lobby at the group of individuals tasting wine at several different tables. Much to his dismay, Logan had decided it was best if they checked into two separate rooms.

After dropping off their bags, they agreed to meet in the lobby. Although Logan was enjoying tasting the different red and white wines available at the winery with the rest of the tourists, he had other thoughts on his mind. Pulling out his smartphone, he hit number one on his speed dial.

"Big brother, to what do I owe this phone call?"

"Sophia, I'm here. What room are you in?"

"Okay, I knew you threatened to follow me, but I really didn't think you would."

"What room are you in?" he repeated firmly.

"I'm actually walking toward you right now."

At the sound of the double echo of her voice, Tristan turned around just as his sister was entering the lobby.

"Don't give me that look," she said as she approached. "Just because you don't want Justice and I together didn't mean fate wouldn't bring us back together anyway."

"Fate," he repeated with a raised eyebrow. "You think fate is what brought you both together?"

"Don't you believe in fate? Or are you too busy letting our parents' failed relationship and the way your ex wronged you do the deciding for you?"

He clenched his jaw at how close his sister had come to the truth. "If Justice really respected you, he would have dated you out in the open instead of keeping you a secret. Then asked our father's permission like he should have."

"News flash, big bro, I was the one who wanted to keep our relationship a secret. And he actually listened to you when you asked him to stay away from me after you found out."

"Sophia," he began, shaking his head, "he's eight years older than you. It's just not right."

"Why?" Sophia questioned as she crossed her arms over her chest. "Because what could a successful, loving, and downright sexy man want with a twenty-four year old who's really just jumpstarting her career?"

"That's not what I meant and you know it." He gave her a stern look when he noticed the diamond ring on her finger for the first time. "I just think that you're too good for him."

"I agree," said a deep voice coming from behind him. "Nice to see you again, Tristan."

He took a deep breath as he regarded the man that used to be one of his closest friends. "I wish I could say the same to you, Justice."

"Oh come on, Tristan, are you really going to act like this?" Sophia asked.

Tristan was about to respond, when he was interrupted.

"Hi, Justice, it's nice to meet you," Logan said as she approached. "My name is Logan Sapphire."

"Nice to meet you, too," Justice replied, staring from Tristan to Logan. Unfortunately, his curious stares were nothing compared to the expression of shock on his sister's face.

"Hi Sophia." Logan leaned forward and gave his sister a quick hug.

"Hey Lo," Sophia said in a surprised voice. "Wait, so you both came down here together?" She waved her finger back and forth between both of them.

"More like your brother forced me to come," Logan explained as she raised both of her eyebrows.

"Sorry," Logan continued as she looked at a confused Justice. "I'm, ah ..." Her voice trailed off as she glanced from Tristan to Sophia. Tristan assumed she was trying to think of an explanation without revealing High Class Society.

"She's a friend of mine," Tristan added. "But back to what's important. Are you both already married?"

"Not yet," Sophia released a frustrated sigh, "but we will be later tonight in a very intimate ceremony. Tristan," she began, gently touching his arm, "two of our close friends are here. I would really love it if for once you didn't pass judgment on our relationship and just supported me in this decision. Maybe even walk me down the aisle?"

"But none of our family is here. They don't even know you ran off with Justice."

"You didn't tell them?" Sophia asked in surprise.

"Only because I didn't want to break Mom's heart by not attending her only daughter's wedding, or hurt Dad for not getting to walk you down the aisle. Did you ever stop to think that starting a marriage with yet another secret, which in this case is a secret ceremony, might not be the best way to go about this?"

She didn't say anything, only stared back at him in response. He looked down at her expectant eyes and didn't try to mask the fact that he was still completely against this decision. *Two of our close friends are here?* From what he knew, they didn't share any mutual friends.

As he stood there observing his sister, he had to admit that he had never seen her look so happy. She'd changed a lot over the years, yet he couldn't remember the last time he just stopped and noticed how much she'd grown. Regardless, she was still his little sister, and although Justice had told him once that Sophia had made him a changed man, Tristan couldn't put aside everything he knew about Justice and his past.

"Actually—" Tristan, who prepared to talk some sense into her yet again, was interrupted again.

"Tristan, can I speak with you?" Logan asked as she looped her arm in his. He met her eyes. "It's okay." She gently touched his chin, obviously picking up on the fact that he was afraid to leave in fear that he wouldn't get a chance to talk to Sophia again. "I don't need long."

Logan turned to Sophia and Justice. "Can you promise us you'll wait here for a couple minutes?" she asked.

Justice and Sophia nodded their heads in agreement, but Tristan didn't miss the knowing smile his sister gave him upon speculating that something more was brewing between him and Logan.

"What's wrong?" he asked when they were on the other side of the lobby and out of earshot.

"Your attitude is what's wrong," Logan replied. "I know you're upset that they are getting married, but you need to try and see this situation through Sophia's eyes."

"Trust me, I understand that she is looking at this through rose-colored glasses."

"That may be so," Logan agreed. "But you told me that even when you and your sister didn't have anyone else, you had each other. Don't you think that this is one of those times when you need to put your feelings aside and be there to support her?"

He ran his fingers down his face letting her words sink in. "I tried being okay with their relationship when I first found out," he replied. "Then I remembered that even though Justice is a good man, he was always a womanizer."

"Well, I haven't heard any rumors like that about him in the past few years. Maybe it's possible that the man you once knew changed when he became serious about pursuing your sister."

As Logan began running her hand up and down his back to relieve his frustration, he wanted to tell her that her hands on him was having the complete opposite effect. Instead, it was soliciting an alert reaction from a body part he needed to remain submissive right now.

"The last thing you want to do is push Sophia away or not be there for her tonight," she said. "Trust me, I think you may regret it, and you don't want her resentment to stand in the way of continuing to build a close relationship with her."

Her voice was so calming in that moment. Probably one of the most soothing voices he'd ever heard.

"Tristan, you're a great man and reasonable when you want to be. I see the part of you that's located in here," she said as she placed her hand over his heart. "That tries to shut people out in fear of getting hurt, when in reality, you believe in love. You want love. Dare I even say … you crave love."

He gazed into the eyes of a woman who in a matter of days, had inched her way beneath his skin and touched him in a place in his heart that had otherwise been untouched.

"Sophia found the one thing that you have spent part of your life searching for, and the last thing I think you want to do is turn your back on her when what she really needs is for her big brother to say everything is going to be okay."

His heartbeat quickened, and from the way she glanced at

her hand placed over his heart, he was sure she could feel it, too. Most people took years to figure him out, yet Logan was making him seem like an open book, which he definitely was not. In that moment, he knew there was no way he would be able to expose High Class Society. Not when one of the women behind the organization was one that he could no longer deny strong feelings for ... despite how crazy it seemed to fall for a woman he'd only just met.

"Okay," he said, taking her hand in his as he led them back to where Sophia and Justice were still standing. When he reached his sister, he gave her a smile.

"What kind of brother would I be if I missed my sister's big day?"

"Thank you so much," Sophia exclaimed as she gave him a big hug.

"Thank you," Justice added, shaking hands with him.

"I don't know what type of magic you worked on my brother," Sophia said when she turned to Logan, "but whatever it is, I hope you tell me the secret."

He glanced over at Logan who offered him a sweet smile. He had to agree with his sister. He hoped Logan would tell him whatever type of magic she was using to make him feel like maybe, just *maybe,* he had found the type of woman who could give him the kind of love he needed.

* * *

STARING at her full body reflection in the mirror, Logan wondered if Tristan would like the way she looked in her blue form-fitting evening dress that she was wearing to Sophia and Justice's wedding.

Even more so, she wondered if he would notice her favorite blue sapphire ring that she was sporting on her right pointer finger. Tonight was the night she was finally going to tell him the truth about everything she'd discovered. She had to admit, she was so nervous she thought she might be sick.

She was so confused about her decision and wasn't sure if she should even say something in the first place. Who knew if he'd even felt the same way about her back when they were just having sex disguised as other people?

"This is insane," she huffed, closing her eyes and willing her heart to stop beating out of her chest. When she heard a firm knock on her door, she was sure it was Tristan even though he was ten minutes earlier than when he'd said he'd stop by.

"Completely nuts," she voiced when she noticed goose bumps form on her arm as she made her way to the door.

The minute she swung open the door, her mouth dried and she forgot to breathe. There he was, standing in a classic black suit, shoes that she recognized as top name brand loafers that she'd pictured in a magazine, and a silver and black watch with two diamonds on either side that glistened so much she couldn't help but run her fingers over the timepiece.

"You are really talented," she said, removing her hand from his wrist. "Maybe one day you can design me a customized watch."

"I didn't think you noticed my watches," he said with smirk. *Notice his watches?* Hell, she noticed every damn thing about him, which is why her stomach had gone from doing summersaults to full-blown three hundred and sixty degree back flips.

"I noticed." When she'd spoken, her voice was a little raspier than she would have liked. Squinting her eyes, she observed the detail of his suit. "Gucci, isn't it?"

"It is," he said, stepping toward her and walking through the door. He didn't need an invite. She wanted him to come in just as badly as he wanted to. When he brushed past her she breathed in his enticing scent. Most men had one main cologne that they normally wore, yet with Tristan there was always a slight difference in the scent. However, what remained regardless of what cologne he wore, was that underlying masculinity that was uniquely his ... That same fragrance drove her insane with lust and forced her to clench her legs together as tightly as she could to soothe the ache.

Tonight, there was a hint of lavender and cedar wood in his scent, and she had no doubt the cologne he was sporting was Gucci Guilty Intense ... the one she couldn't get enough of after she'd smelled it in Macy's.

When she turned around to face him, her skin tingled with awareness as she watched him appraise her dress. The way he was looking at her legs made her feel slightly weak in the knees.

Within seconds, his arms wrapped around her waist and pulled her to the fit of him.

"I've been waiting to do this all day," he said, lifting her onto the side table against the wall as his lips descended to hers. The moment she felt his hands slide up her thighs, she lost all ability to think.

He wasted no time finding her scanty panties and pushing them inside to dip his fingers into her warmth. She arched her back upon contact, and the movement allowed him to push his fingers even deeper inside her. He began pumping with exact precision, hitting her g-spot every time.

Although his thighs were positioned in such a way that she didn't think she could slip off the table, she gripped his biceps for support anyway.

"Tristan," she whispered as a warning that she was on the brink of releasing her orgasm. His fingers increased their movements gaining another moan from her. He wouldn't let up. She didn't want him to let up. This game they were playing was a dangerous one because as far as Logan was concerned, her heart was involved. But if this had to be it between them, she wasn't going out without familiarizing herself with another part of his body that she hadn't seen up close and personal yet.

When she finally released her orgasm, she allowed herself to relish in the moment for a few seconds before she gathered all of her strength and pushed on his chest so she could get off the table.

She smiled at the look of confusion on his face before she took his arm and led him over to the king-sized bed. She glanced at the clock on the nightstand. "We have six minutes before we have to leave so that we won't be too late," she said as she began unbuckling his pants before removing them carefully to avoid wrinkles, and unbuttoning his dress shirt for the sole purpose of ogling his abs. He was already straining against his zipper, and he managed to nod his head in agreement.

After he was free of confinement, she sauntered on the bed, admiring his dick the entire way up his glorious body. There was nothing sexier than an aroused man who was willing and ready to do whatever you wanted to do. And boy was she ready to make his toes curl in excitement.

She leaned down ran her tongue over the tip for a quick tease. The reaction she received encouraged her to run her tongue over him once more before she slowly eased her mouth over him. He hit the hilt of her throat, and even then she tried to suck him in even more.

"Damn," he groaned loudly, watching her slow perusal of his length the entire time. She continued to suck him in her own unique rhythm, satisfied that he was getting to the point of no return.

When she added her hand movements to match the movement of her mouth, she purposely used the hand that was sporting her blue sapphire ring. Just as she'd hoped, even blinded by lust, his eyes locked in on her ring before shooting to her face and mouth, which was still devouring every delicious bit of him.

"I've seen that before," he said in a hoarse voice.

"Have you?" Logan asked in-between licks. She thought she'd heard him respond again, but the quickening of her tongue and tightening of her jaw muscles caused him to throw his head back to the pillow. She smiled, knowing he wasn't ready for what she had in store next.

Adjusting herself on her knees, she lifted his shaft and cupped his testicles in her hand, making sure she gave them a quick massage before she went to the next step.

She glanced up at his expectant eyes, a part of him looking like he knew what might come next and the other part of him questioning if she was really going to do the move that he thought she was.

Up until now, Logan had done a really good job of not repeating some of the familiar looks with her eyes that she'd remembered doing in the past when she was sexually aroused. Now, it was finally the perfect moment to flash her eyes and facial movements in a way that she always did when she was Blue and he was Hunter. That naughty look right before she rocked his world.

She bent down, her head slowly easing between his thighs. She found the spot right underneath his balls, the spot that drove him crazy, and massaged that spot before taking one of his balls into her mouth. She alternated her sucking techniques between each testicle, making sure she switched between massaging them as well. When his groans grew louder, proof that he didn't have that much longer, she placed her tongue at his base and ran her tongue up and down his length. In the past, after she'd already gotten him close to the brink, ten complete licks had been his capping point.

Tonight, she'd only gotten to five when she felt his entire body tense with pleasure. When he released himself in one of the biggest orgasms she'd ever remembered him having after oral sex, she sucked him dry, making sure she didn't leave one last drop.

"Fuckkk," he said drawing out the word as he ran his hand down his face after his convulsions began to subside. She'd brought him even deeper than he probably thought possible, and the expression on his face now was one she was sure she'd never forget. He looked sexy—he looked ready to take her to bed—but what really caught her attention, were the questions that he was evidently trying to answer.

She sat back on her legs and waited for him to ask her something … anything. However, he remained silent as he observed her with confusion. Definitely not the response she was searching for.

"You look like you want to ask me something," she said when she realized he wasn't going to speak anytime soon. "About us and what just happened."

He searched her eyes, but as quickly as the look of confusion had come, it left. "What I want to do to you doesn't require us talking," he replied as he pulled her on top of him. She studied his eyes, disappointed that he seemed to dismiss whatever familiarity he had been feeling before. There was no way he hadn't made the connection. The way she'd sucked his dick had been a signature move of hers, and if that wasn't a clue, the ring she was sporting on her finger should have been.

The thought briefly crossed her mind that maybe he didn't have anything to ask her because he did make the connection and didn't want to acknowledge it. If that was the case, it still felt like some backhand rejection and she didn't like the feeling.

She was so wrapped up in his reaction that she'd barely

heard the knock on the door until Tristan had mentioned it to her. Rising from the bed, she adjusted her dress before making her way to the door, determined to tell housekeeping or whomever it was to leave.

"What's wrong?" Logan asked when she opened the door to an emotional Sophia.

"The wedding's off," Sophia answered as she wiped a few more tears from her eyes. Remembering that Tristan was in her room barely dressed, Logan stepped out into the hallway and let the door close behind her.

"What happened, sweetie?"

"Justice said he didn't want to marry me. I don't think he loves me anymore. I tried to make this work, but clearly after two years of waiting to marry me, he's moved on."

"What?" Logan rubbed her hands up and down Sophia's shoulders in attempt to calm her. "I saw the way he was looking at you, and he definitely seems like a man in love."

"Just not with me," Sophia said between sobs.

"What happened?" Tristan asked, opening the door. Sophia glanced from both of them before a few more tears fell down her face.

"I didn't know you were here. I wasn't ready to face you yet and hear I told you so," Sophia said to Tristan as she wiped her eyes. "You were right. Justice called off the wedding. He said maybe we weren't supposed to be together after all."

When Tristan curled his hands into a fist, Logan gently placed her hands on each fist and shook her head. "Now is not the time to find him and pick a fight," she whispered to him. "Focus on Sophia first."

Tristan pulled Sophia in for a hug. "I'm so sorry if this was my fault."

"It wasn't just you," she said, breaking off the hug. "I

honestly don't know what it was. Maybe I was forcing him to do something he no longer wanted to do."

Sophia glanced between Logan and Tristan again. "I obviously interrupted something between you guys so I'll just head back to my room."

"She needs you now more than ever," Logan stated after Sophia had left them alone. "Go talk to her. I'll be fine. We'll continue this conversation some other time." *And by some other time, I mean never.*

"Okay," he said, kissing her cheek. "I'll come back to your room later tonight." Logan waited until he had left to respond.

"And I'll already be checked out," she whispered before walking over to her suitcase to pack the few items she had unpacked. She didn't think it would be the last time she saw Tristan—especially since they still had the matter of him outing her company to attend to—but with any luck, she could forget about tonight and how she'd made a fool of herself.

"Highly unlikely," she said, already thinking about the nice bottle of red wine that was waiting for her when she got home.

She was packed and ready to go within thirty minutes. After checking out and having the front desk call a cab, she decided to wait outside to avoid running into Tristan despite the cold chill brought on by the night weather.

"Seems I'm not the only one running," a voice said to the left of her just past the light post.

She squinted her eyes in the darkness. "Justice, is that you?"

"Yes, it's me," he answered miserably.

Logan walked over to him thinking he sounded as terrible as Sophia had. "I should slap you for what you're putting Sophia through," she said, unable to hide her disappointment.

"Do it. I'm sure I deserve it."

She looked at him intuitively. "Why did you call off the wedding?"

"It's complicated," he stated.

"Don't you love her?"

"Of course I do," he said in a defensive tone. "This doesn't have anything to do with love."

"Then what does it have to do with?" Logan asked.

"You wouldn't possibly understand."

Logan observed his body language. The defeat in his features was hard to miss. Justice Covington may be every woman's fantasy, but from what Logan knew from the file HCS had on him, he'd had a tough childhood. She sensed that there was something deeper going on, but she didn't know him well enough to pry. Even so, her curiosity and concern for Sophia wouldn't let her leave him alone.

"Try me. You'd be surprised at how much I understand."

CHAPTER 12

"Okay, although I adore the fact that you're so concerned with my well-being," Sophia said, "don't you think it's best if you finally talk to Logan?"

Tristan glanced away from the television to look at his sister. "What do you mean?" he asked. "I told you to tell her assistant that I wouldn't be exposing HCS. I even signed that confidentiality agreement she sent over. What else could I possibly have to say to her?"

"Oh, I don't know," Sophia replied, clasping her hands together. "How about the fact that you love her."

"I barely know her."

"Yet you love her all the same." Sophia got up from the chair she was sitting on to join him on the couch. "Listen, I admit that my heart took a hard beating, but that doesn't mean yours has to as well. Even though it was a little over a week ago, I can still recall the way you both were looking at each other in Napa Valley. It was almost as if you hadn't just met. Those feelings seemed real."

Oh how close you are to the truth, he thought as he turned his attention back to the sports game. It hadn't taken long

103

after he'd discovered that Logan had left Napa for all of the signs that had been thrown in his face to come back and slap him across the head.

Throughout their entire time together, he'd kept thinking about the fact that Logan seemed a lot like his mystery woman. The one he'd fallen for without even knowing her real name. The one he'd refused to believe had left him high and dry, forcing him to refrain from the Friday night secret sex acts that he'd become so accustomed to because nothing was the same without Blue.

Despite their similarities, he'd thought there was no way in hell Blue and Logan were the same woman, but after that night she'd gone down on him and he'd spotted her blue sapphire ring, he'd known the truth was staring him in the face all along. There was only one woman who could make him feel that good. One who could work her tongue and mouth unlike any woman he'd ever been with before. The realization that he'd spent five Fridays in a row searching for Blue, only to walk right into her office and stumble upon the woman he was never able to forget, had been too much for him to handle at the time. He had honestly planned on talking to her before his sister interrupted them, but he'd wanted to make love to her first and show her how he felt just in case his voice failed to say the words.

"Tristan," his sister called, regaining his attention, "I don't know what went wrong that night I came to Logan's hotel room, and if it was my fault, I apologize. But if you love her or care about her at all, I suggest you go to her and tell her before another man comes into her life and realizes how amazing she is."

He thought about the possibility of Logan being with someone else and realized that whether she was Logan, Blue, Lo, or some other secret name that he had yet to learn, he couldn't imagine her being with anyone but him.

"It's time for you to stop letting your past determine your future," Sophia added.

Taking a deep breath, he thought about her words that mirrored how he'd already been feeling for the past week and a half.

"You're right," Tristan said as he stood from the couch. "I just hope when I get to the HCS office she'll allow me to see her."

"Aww, Tristan, you're growing up."

"What do you mean?"

"You're finally following your heart instead of your head. I've been telling you to do that for years. And as far as getting into the HCS office, I think I can help with that."

* * *

"Seriously, guys, I don't need an intervention," Logan said to her fellow High Class Society founders, Savannah Westbrook, Harper Rose, and Peyton Davis.

"Yes you do," Harper stated as she leaned her hip against Logan's office desk. "You've been moping around for the past few days, and it's pretty obvious that you miss Tristan."

She ran her tongue across her teeth in irritation. "I do not mope. In order to mope, I'd have to have lost him when quite the contrary, I never had him in the first damn place."

"And you've been cursing like a sailor," Savannah said in a cautious tone.

"And you're downright bitchy lately," Peyton added.

"I don't even know why I told you guys about him." Logan dropped her head back to stare at the ceiling. When she'd arrived back to New York and tried to continue working as if nothing had happened, her friends had instantly known that something was wrong. Once her assistant informed her that Tristan had agreed to sign the confidently agreement, she felt it best to let the ladies know what had been going on. Since Jade was on the Board of Directors for High Class Society, her partners knew Jade's organization provided the naughty Friday nights, but they'd had no idea Logan had participated until she came clean after she'd divulged the entire story about Tristan.

"Did you ever think that maybe fate brought you and Tristan together? Perhaps, instead of dropping hints and expecting him to pick up on them, you should tell him how you feel straight out," Harper said. "Every day we encourage women in our organization to go after the men they want. Yet, you haven't taken that same advice."

"And the Logan we know wouldn't have left that hotel without telling him how you feel," Savannah chimed in.

Logan pretended to get engrossed in straightening some knick-knacks on her desk. They were right and she knew it. She'd spent the past week and half wondering why she hadn't just come right out and tell Tristan how she felt. Especially, since she wasn't the type to hold back her thoughts or feelings.

But that was the funny thing about rejection. Once you've experienced the feeling, it had a way of creeping up on you when you least expected it. She may not let it define her, but somewhere in her psyche, she'd decided that she had to approach Tristan with caution for fear of repeating past mistakes.

As she glanced up at her friends and really let their words sink in, she realized that she owed it to herself to be the confident go-getter she was known for and tell Tristan how she felt whether he liked it or not.

"Okay, ladies," she said, getting up from her desk chair, "time for me to handle this situation."

"By handle, do you mean that you're finally going to talk to Tristan?" Savannah asked in a hopeful tone.

"That's exactly what I mean." She grabbed her black pea coat and purse before heading to her office door. "He may not want to hear what the hell I have to say, but I've always been a sharp shooter so it's time for him to listen."

"What if I have something that I need you to listen to first?"

Logan stopped dead in her tracks at the sound of the deep baritone voice blocking her office doorway.

"You know, this whole battle of the words thing is really getting old," she stated.

He gave her sly smile … the one where his lips curled to one side in such a sexy way. "I beg to differ," he said as he stepped closer to her.

"Of course you do." Even in her heels, she had to tilt her head slightly to look up at him. Scanning his face, she noticed a few tired lines around his eyes that hadn't been there before. *Is there a chance he's losing sleep over me, like I'm losing over him?* She hadn't had a good night's sleep since they'd parted, and now that Tristan was standing right in front of her, she realized even more how she missed being around him.

His eyes dropped to her lips, and the hungry look reflected in them made her want to scream for him to steal as many kisses as he wanted as long as he promised to let her devour him just as eagerly. He must have read the dirty direction her thoughts were headed because his penetrating eyes seemed to grow even darker.

The sound of someone clearing their throat behind her, made Logan turn to the friends she'd forgotten were still in the room.

"Hello, ladies," Tristan said, addressing the women for the first time.

"Oh, don't mind us," Harper waved her hands for them to

continue, "we'll just stand here and watch you both make love with your eyes."

Savannah nudged Harper while Peyton just smiled.

"Nina said I could come right in," Tristan explained, reclaiming her attention. "Is it okay for us to talk?"

"Sure," Logan said, nodding for her friends to exit her office. After a few seconds, they left ... but not before they each whispered a few words of encouragement in her ear.

"So," he began as he clasped his hands together, "although my sister and I stayed in Napa for a couple days and had a real heart to heart, it took me about an hour after you left to realize something."

"And what might that be?" she asked, trying to keep her voice calm when in reality, she felt like her heart was beating in her throat.

He took a step closer to her. "That there was no way I could let you walk out of my life the same way you did a few months ago."

Logan let out a breath she hadn't been aware she was holding. "When did you figure it out?" she asked, searching his eyes.

"I think if I'm honest with myself, I suspected it right after we shared that first kiss. But I thought there was no way in hell I was actually right about my assumptions."

"I felt the same way," she stated, finally releasing some tension from her body. "I didn't think it was possible that you were my mystery man. The idea seemed too far-fetched."

She took a few steps back so that she could prop one thigh on her desk for support. His eyes followed the movement of her navy skirt rising up her thighs just as he had when he'd walked into her office a couple of weeks ago, and she smiled to herself.

"So why did you stop meeting me on Friday nights?" His voice seemed slightly guarded when he asked the question.

She studied his features, knowing that the time had finally come for her to tell him why she'd ended their affair.

"Because somewhere between you consuming every inch of my body and exploring parts of me that no man had ever taken the time to discover, I began losing my heart in the process."

"And that was a bad thing?" he asked, pinning her with a look that warned her that saying yes was not the correct answer.

"Developing feelings was never part of the game plan," she said instead.

"No, it wasn't," he agreed before his face grew more serious, "but the only reason I enjoyed those Friday nights was because I knew Blue would be there, and she'd be as anxious to see me as I was to see her."

She smiled. "So it began to mean more to you, too?"

"More like it began to mean *everything* to me," he told her sincerely. Upon hearing that her feelings weren't one-sided, a wave of satisfaction washed over her.

"You know I have to ask," he began in a teasing tone as he crossed his arms over his chest, "but is there is a third secret society you're a part of that I should know about?"

She fidgeted with her fingers. "Well, there is one other …" Her voice trailed off and she laughed at his upturned eyebrow. "Just kidding." Grinning, she raised her hands in defeat. "I only belong to two secret organizations. That's all."

"Then how about we start over?" he asked as he extended his hand. "Hi, my name is Tristan Derrington. And you are?"

"Hello, Tristan, my name is Logan Sapphire." She laughed as she stood from her desk and accepted his outreached hand.

"It's nice to meet you, Logan." When he pulled her closer to him, his scent wafted through her nostrils.

"Is that Armani cologne that you're wearing?"

"You know your scents well," he said with a side smile.

"More like I know my suit brands well. You're wearing an Armani suit, aren't you?"

He shook his head and laughed. "Yes I am."

"I knew I had to be right from the minute you stepped into my office," she sighed in appreciation.

"Right about my suit or my cologne?"

She ran her fingers down the collar of his suit. "Right about the fact that you wear the same brand of cologne to match whatever suit brand you're sporting. When you first walked in my office, you had on a Tom Ford suit, and I definitely didn't miss that enticing brand of Tom Ford cologne you were wearing. Then, in my hotel room that night you were wearing a Gucci suit and Gucci cologne. Today, an Armani suit and Armani cologne."

He squinted his eyes in surprise, before pinning her with an intense look. "No one has ever picked up on that before."

She gave him a slight smile, suddenly feeling bashful under his observation. He had a way of doing that to her … making her feel empowered, yet shy at the same time. It wasn't his words that made her feel that way, but rather a combination of his words and the way he looked at her. "There isn't much about you that I don't notice," she admitted.

"I see." He gently brushed the bottom of her chin with his hand. "Just like I notice how you bite the side of your lip when you're thinking really hard about something. Or the way you squint your eyes and tilt your head to the side right before you ask someone a serious question. Or even funnier, how you play with your fingers right before you're about to lie about something."

His arms wrapped around her waist. "But there is so much more I want to tell you that I notice about you. So,

Logan, I'd like to take you out on our first official date," he said. "Would that be something you'd be interested in?"

"And what exactly are we going to do on this first date?" she asked as she curled her arms around his neck.

"This may be too forward," he murmured as he got closer to her right ear, "but as long as our date ends with you naked on my sheets and spread on all fours, I don't give a damn what we do."

"I assure you, I wouldn't have it any other way," she said, and placed her lips on his to demonstrate her promise.

EPILOGUE

*ne month later ...*

"Back where it all started. What's the theme for tonight?" Tristan asked Logan as he glanced around while they made their way through the long, dark, narrow hallway.

"Tonight is Face Down Friday."

"Oh shit," he said, wrapping his arms around her waist. "I don't know how others are interpreting it, but there's nothing more I'd rather do than use my tongue to deep dive in that sweet sea of yours."

"You're so nasty," she told him with a laugh.

"And you love it," he replied. He twisted her around to face him and slowly twirled her until they were in a dimly lit room with a flashing blue light in the top corner.

"Are you sure you don't want to find a room further down the hall?" she asked breathlessly. Tristan was already sliding her black lace panties down her thighs with such force that she was surprised he didn't snap them off.

"I can't wait that long," he said with a groan before he locked the door and closed the blinds. Each room had an option to keep the blinds open so that people walking down the hall could view you or closed for your privacy. In the past, Blue and Hunter had always kept the blinds closed. However, now that they knew each other as Logan and Tristan, it was time for a change.

"Let's keep the blinds open this time," she whispered into his ear. His head flew to hers as he gazed into her eyes. They were covered in body paint and both wearing masks so their identities would still be kept a secret. But the thrill of being watched was something Logan had always wanted to do.

Tristan went over to the blinds and opened them back up, his eyes never leaving hers.

"Is there ever anything you'll do that won't surprise me?"

"Now where's the fun in that?" she teased with a sly smile. Making her way to the circular bed located in the middle of the room against the wall, she seductively unclipped her matching black lace bra and tossed it to the side to join her panties.

"Come here," she said as she crooked her finger to Tristan. Not to be outdone, he took his time walking toward her. When he reached the bed, she licked her lips at the way the black briefs hugged his thighs and accented his v line. He discarded his briefs, but instead of joining her on the bed, he twisted her so that she was facing the wall, placed her hands above her head, and began tying her wrists to a bar above the bed.

She'd noticed a long, black satin sash hanging from his neck, but she'd assumed it was part of the dark and dangerous look he was going for tonight. She'd had no idea he was using the material to restrain her.

"I'm not sure I like this," she called over her shoulder with a sexy smile. "It's supposed to be Face Down Friday, yet I can't bend my head down if I'm tied up like this."

"Like I said before," he said, squeezing a hard nipple. "I'm interpreting this theme a little differently, but I guarantee my head will be down."

She didn't have a chance to respond before his hands pushed her thighs apart in a move that caught her off guard. Within seconds, she looked down between her legs and saw his head appear beneath her.

"Oh I see," she said breathlessly.

"I knew you would." He suddenly grabbed her thighs and pulled her onto his mouth. Within seconds, she was panting and throwing back her head in purring moans that filled the small room. Her hips began to ride his tongue, and she couldn't resist another glance over her shoulder. She couldn't see his entire body, but she was able to view his appetizing abs flexing with every movement of his tongue, and his muscular thighs glistening with sweat, proof that even orally, he was putting in work. Not only that, but his erection willing and ready to be a participant in their sexual tryst as soon as he finished demonstrating *exactly* what he felt about Face Down Friday.

"It seems we have an audience," she voiced when she glanced at the window and saw several men and woman viewing what they were doing. And from the looks of it, more than a couple were getting off at the sight.

"Let them look," he said between licks. "Because I'm not stopping until you give me exactly what I need."

She didn't have to ask what that was because she was within seconds of giving him just that. As if on cue, her panting became more rapid and her hips began moving over his tongue even faster. She wanted to move her hands or grip the wall—any damn thing to help her deal with the brunt force of the orgasm she knew was coming—but he knew what he was doing when he'd tied her up. Therefore, she had no choice but to enjoy the sweetest type of torture.

A few more suckles of her clit and she exploded in his mouth just as hard as she'd predicted. Her hips bucked from the intensity, but Tristan didn't seem to care one bit. He lapped up every bit of her pussy juice, and then had the nerve to dip two fingers inside of her as if her orgasm wasn't enough proof that she was hot and ready for him.

To her enjoyment, he untied her wrists, twisted her around, and slid her lower on to the bed so that she was positioned right beneath him.

Forgotten were the people viewing them at the window because the only thing she had eyes for was Tristan. The look on his face proved that she was in for the ride of her life, and if she was reading him correctly, he definitely didn't only mean for tonight.

When he finally slid inside of her, the feeling of complete and utter satisfaction consumed every part of her.

He inched his face closer to hers and brushed his hand across her cheek. "I don't know what you did to me, but I am deeply and unconditionally in love with you, Logan Sapphire."

She studied his eyes and was overcome with emotion at the love and devotion reflected in them. He'd chosen the word unconditionally, not doubt implying that he loved her for who she was ... Logan Sapphire, a woman who wasn't perfect and one who had a father who was still in jail for the crimes he committed ... A woman who had graduated at the top of her class at Yale despite those who felt like she wasn't in the right social class to ever be a real success ... A woman who had fought hard to rise to the top of her company despite the adversity she had to overcome ... A woman who had been hurt by her ex-husband's rejection and afraid to give her heart to any man again.

"I am so in love with you, too, Tristan Derrington," she whispered as she dragged his head to hers in a passionate kiss. He hadn't just opened up her heart in ways she'd never imagined; he was living proof that in High Class Society Incorporated, love may find you when you least expect it. And *that* was why her friends and fellow founders fought so hard for their members ... their friends ... their *sisterhood*.

WOULD LOVE TO HEAR FROM YOU!

I hope you enjoyed Blue Sapphire Temptation! Make sure you check out the remaining books in the series!

Series Order (www.HighClassSocietyInc.com):

Blue Sapphire Temptation, Book 1 - Logan "Lo"

Her Sweetest Seduction, Book 2 - Savannah

Sealed with a Kiss, Book 3 - Peyton

Passionate Persuasion, Book 4 - Harper

Stop by my online Coffee Corner and get the latest info on my books, contests, events and more!

www.bit.ly/SherelleGreensCoffeeCorner

Also, authors love to hear from readers! Thanks in advance for any reviews, messages or emails :). Keep turning for more goodies!

Save and Author! Leave a Review!

ONCE UPON A BRIDESMAID SERIES

When four bridesmaids come together to support their best friend's wedding, they realize that most of the people they know have already tied the knot. Whether unlucky in love or single by choice, these besties make a pact to change their relationship status. The goal is simple... Each woman has one year to find Mr. Right and say 'I do'. Between passionate one-night-stands and best friend hookups, these bridesmaids are in for a wild ride. Are they in over their heads? Or will one impulsive wedding pact change their lives... forever.

Yours Forever excerpt on next page

Yours Forever by Sherelle Green (Book 1)

Beyond Forever by Elle Wright (Book 2)

Embracing Forever by Sheryl Lister (Book 3)

Hopelessly Forever by Angela Seals (Book 4)

EXCERPT: YOURS FOREVER

The Pact

There are two things in life that a woman always needs to have in her possession: her sanity and her punani. Grandma Pearl's words echoed in Mackenzie Cannon's mind as she fidgeted in her cushioned wicker chair and ignored the conversation taking place between her best friends.

Grandma Pearl had always been one of Mac's favorite people. Not only had she been a classy woman with her large church hats and beautiful thick figure, but she'd also been the one to teach Mac the art of talking dirty without it sounding dirty.

Granted, there were times that Mac would rather say *pussy* instead of *punani*, but she kept it as classy as she could.

"I bet he tastes as good as he looks," Mac said aloud, taking in the delicious sight of the best man in a tux. "Can someone please get me a glass of water?"

When he turned to look her way, she didn't even try to hide her thorough perusal of his body. Now that one of her best friends was married and dancing with her new husband on the dance floor, Mac could loosen her bridesmaid dress and focus on the tall cup of coffee who'd held her attention all weekend long.

"Seriously, Mac! Are you even listening to what I'm saying?"

Mac turned to face her best friend since childhood, Quinn Jacobs. They may be polar opposites, but Mac had a soft spot for Q. Despite their differences, they were extremely close. "I heard you, Q. I agree, Ava and Owen look happy. But in case you didn't notice, I'm trying my best focus on something a little more interesting than the newlyweds."

Mac, Quinn, Raven Emerson, and Ryleigh Fields had grown up in the small town of Rosewood Heights, South Carolina and had been friends since they were little girls. Although they each decided to pursue careers in other states, the women had returned to their hometown to celebrate the union of the fifth member of their pack—and the only friend still residing in Rosewood—Ava Prescott, to her husband, Owen Sullivan. The beautiful wedding had taken place in Rosewood Estates, a staple in the small lake town and perfect for a woman who valued tradition and community like Ava did.

"Why must you be so rude?" Raven asked, shaking her head. "You know how Q gets when she's talking about romance."

"Ha!" Mac said with a laugh. "Anyone within a thirty-mile radius can hear her squeal when she starts talking about love and shit."

"Girl, you can say that again," Ryleigh said, giving Mac a high-five. It was normal for Ryleigh and Mac to agree. Both were headstrong and loved cozying up to a good-looking man every once and a while. At their high school dances, they'd often place bets on who could get the most numbers. Typically, they both took turns winning.

Quinn cleared her throat. "If everyone's done making fun of me, can we please continue the discussion?"

Mac turned her body in her chair so that she could face each of the women just as the waiter approached to take their drink order.

"I'll have another mojito," Mac said as she polished off her third glass in preparation for her fourth. When it came to getting through weddings, Mac had a firm drinking rule... More booze equaled more fun.

Conversation flowed between the friends as if it hadn't been a while since they'd last seen each other. Living in different states meant a lot of emails, calls, and text messages passed between them. Despite the different area codes, they made an effort to have a group conference call at least once a month to stay in touch.

The young waiter returned with their drinks and shot her what she assumed was his killer smile. Mac barely paid the youngin' any mind.

"I think we should toast," Quinn said, lifting her margarita high. "Here's to us all finding that special someone and saying 'I do' by this time next year."

Raven froze, her glass in mid-air. "Are you *crazy*?"

"Oh hell no," Ryleigh said at the same time, almost spilling her drink when she placed her glass on the table.

Mac was shaking her head in disagreement before Quinn even got out the last word. "The only thing I'm saying 'I do' to is one night with that tall, mouth-watering best man standing over there." She glanced over her shoulder in his direction.

Quinn placed her glass down and perked up in her chair. "Oh, come on you guys! We're twenty-nine years old! I don't want to be pushing a stroller when I'm fifty."

"If Janet Jackson can do it, so can we," Mac said with a smile.

"I'm being serious." Quinn scooted forward in her chair. "Think about it. Just about everybody we know has gotten married in the last three years, yet we're all still single. Wouldn't it be nice to have a warm, hard body to snuggle up to every night? To not have to worry about those awkward bar or club meetings? I mean, how hard could it be?" She lifted her glass again. "Come on! We can do this. Right here. Right now. Let's make a pact. Better yet, let's make this a best friend challenge."

Mac winced. *Damn, Q just said the magic words.* They were known to place a wager on anything and Mac *hated* to lose. Mac watched Raven slowly lift her glass to Quinn's. A quick glance at Ryleigh proved that she shared the same sentiment as Mac, but she slowly began to lift her glass as well.

"Oh shit," Mac huffed. "Are you seriously trying to make us all agree to be married before this time next year?"

Quinn smirked. "I thought the *Queen of Friends with Benefits* wasn't afraid of anything."

Mac rolled her eyes at the not-so-endearing nickname her friends had given her back when they were in high school. "I'm not afraid of anything."

"Then raise your glass, girlfriend," Quinn teased.

Mac hesitantly bit her bottom lip before finally raising her glass.

"To finding that special someone and saying 'I do' by this time next year," Quinn repeated when all four glasses were raised.

Mac felt like she was on auto-pilot as they clinked glasses before taking a sip of their drinks. *Screw it,* she thought as she downed her entire drink after a few more seconds. There weren't too many things that left Mac speechless, but agreeing to this pact was one for the books. *I definitely need a distraction now*, she thought as her eyes drifted back to the best man.

Mac stood from her chair. "Well, ladies, as fun as this is, I'll have to catch you in the morning for breakfast."

Quinn shook her head. "You won't find your husband by getting in the best man's pants."

Mac smoothed out her bridesmaid dress. "Sweetie, I'm sure my future husband, whomever he may be, will appreciate my sex drive. In the meantime, there are other men who will appreciate it just as much."

Was Mac ashamed that she enjoyed sex so much? Absolutely not. Would Mac ever apologize for having a frivolous fling? No way! She knew who she was and she didn't have to explain herself to anybody.

Quinn shook her head. "It's not always about sex, Mac."

"And marriage isn't always about love and romance." With a wink, Mac made her way across the room, leaving her friends to discuss how shocked they were that she'd agreed to the pact. They were probably assuming she would back out, but there was no way Mac was backing down from a best friend challenge. No way at all.

***

"Beware, my brother. You may have been tempted before, but temptation never looked like that."

Alexander Carter followed his brother's gaze, only to find the sexy bridesmaid that he'd been avoiding all weekend walking toward them. *Damn.* It was almost like she'd been plucked from every fantasy he'd ever had of the opposite sex. Her thick honey-brown curls were pulled to the side, cascading over her shoulders. Alex had always had a thing for big, natural curls and hers were no exception. His fingers itched to run through her hair.

If that wasn't enough to send his libido into overdrive, the woman had enough curves to keep a man occupied for decades. While some men always went after the skinny-model type, Alex preferred a woman with a little more meat on her bones. *And damned if she isn't stacked in all the right places.*

He cleared his throat before leaning against the bar and looking back at his younger brother, Shane. "Yeah, I'm in trouble."

"I told you, big bruh, you were in trouble the minute we went to Ava and Owen's luncheon a couple of days ago. When Owen asked us to be in the wedding last year, he warned you that Ava had some fine-ass friends."

"Yeah, but I didn't think he meant any of them were my type."

Shane laughed. "You know Owen has always been into talking in riddles and shit. He was trying to warn you without saying those exact words."

Alex shook his head. "I've been celibate for two years and haven't given into temptation. There's no way I'm giving in now."

Shane's voice lowered. "Listen, I know the face of a woman on a mission, so you have to ask yourself one question. Can you handle denying yourself a night with a sexy siren like her?"

"Yes, I can."

Shane could barely conceal his grin. "Then good luck, my brother." He glanced over Alex's shoulder. "You're gonna need it."

Shane had only been gone two seconds when she approached. "Hello, mind if I join you?"

Alex turned to face the stunning brown beauty he'd just been speaking about. *Tell her no. Send her on her way. You may have had the strength to avoid women before, but not a woman like her.*

"Sure, please do." Her thigh grazed his as she leaned next

to him against the bar. Alex briefly shut his eyes. *Wrong move, my dude.*

"So, what is Alexander Carter's drink of choice?"

He took a sip of his once-forgotten drink. "Cognac on the rocks."

She squinted her eyes. "Smooth, strong, dark. At first it appears simple, but then you take one sip and experience the added element of charm and power." She looked him up and down. "I can see why you like it. It suits you."

Alex grinned slyly. "And what does Miss Mackenzie Cannon drink?"

"Today, mojitos were my drink of choice. But, usually, I'm a White Russian kind of woman."

Alex leaned slightly forward. "A White Russian... Sweet, yet robust. Creamy. The type of drink that sneaks up on you." He observed her a little closer. "And the coffee gives the drink a hint of the unexpected and plays with your taste buds."

When her eyes briefly danced with amusement, Alex noticed they were the color of sweet honey. He licked his lips and her eyes followed the movement.

"Very intuitive, Mr. Carter," Mac said as she stepped a little closer. "I'm not the type of woman to beat around the bush, so I must warn you that I came over here to try and seduce you."

Alex swallowed. "Well, I must say that you're doing a damn good job."

"Oh, I don't know about that, Mr. Carter." She pushed a few of her curls over her shoulder and placed one hand on her hip. "Although I came over here to do the seducing, you're seducing me in ways that you probably don't even realize."

Man, she needs to stop calling me Mr. Carter. Her voice was sultry and as smooth as velvet. Addressing him so formally was only making his pants tighter in the crotch area.

"Want to take a walk?" Mac asked.

If you leave the confides of this reception, you may not be able to control yourself. "Sure," he responded, ignoring the warning.

It was a beautiful September day in Rosewood Heights and Alex found the laid-back lake town extremely relaxing for a city boy like himself.

"I never thought I'd say this, but I miss this small town." Alex glanced at Mac just as she waved to a store owner across the street.

"I can understand why you miss it. I moved around so much as a kid that I don't really have roots anywhere. At least I didn't until I became an adult and settled down on the east coast."

"I know the feeling," Mac said with a laugh. "My family moved around a lot when I was younger, but for some reason, we always came back to Rosewood. And every time we returned, my girlfriends welcomed me back with open arms."

Alex smiled. He hadn't known Mac for more than forty-eight hours, but he'd pegged her as the type that didn't open up easily. The fact that she'd even told him that much surprised him.

They fell into easy conversation with an underline of flirtation in every word they said to one another. As much as Alex missed having sex, he missed the act of flirting even more. In his experience, flirting with a woman meant it would lead to other things. Things of the sexual nature. Things that wouldn't end well for a guy who'd made a vow of celibacy.

"I've done a lot of traveling, but this is still one of my favorite spots," Mac said as they approached a small garden with locks all along the fence. "We call this Love's Last

Garden. It's been said that Rosewood Heights is the place where people come to relax and find love. Most of it is a myth, but this was the last garden that was built in the town and many townsfolk fell in love in this very place. Once you find love, you place a lock on the fence."

Alex looked around at the lush greenery and locks positioned about the fence. He couldn't quite place his finger on it, but he felt even more connected with Mac being in this garden. When he turned back to Mac, his eyes met hers. Watching him. Observing him. She bit her lip again in the same way he'd seen her do all day before her eyes dropped to his lips. *What is it with this woman?* He barely knew her, yet something about her drew him in. And without dwelling on his next move, he took two short strides toward her and pulled her to him.

He gave her a few seconds to protest, but when she looked up at him expectantly, he brought his lips down to hers. Alex had meant for it to be a simple kiss, but he should have known that Mac would awaken a desire deep within him, especially after the tension between them all weekend. She slowly opened her mouth and he took the invitation to add his tongue to the foreplay.

Kissing Mac wasn't what he'd expected. It was so much more. He may be celibate, but he'd had his fair share of kisses. With Mac, she kissed with her entire body, nipping and suckling in a way that was mentally breaking down the walls he usually had up. When her moan drifted to his ears, Alex pulled her even closer, tilting her head for better access. His hands eventually found their way to her ass, cupping her through the material of her dress. Although the sun had set, they kissed in a way that made Alex forget that they were standing in a public garden.

At her next moan, Alex stepped back. *Man, you need to get a grip.* Even with the space between them, he could still feel her heat. If she kissed like that, he could only imagine how she'd be in bed.

They stood there for a couple of minutes, neither saying anything as they took in their fill of one another. Being the CEO of an environmental engineer firm, Alex knew a thing or two about self-control to reach the ultimate goal. He was one of the most controlled people he knew. However, as he got lost in Mac's honey gaze, he couldn't remember the reasons why he'd decided to be celibate in the first place. *Surely there were a list of reasons, right?*

Mac stepped back to him and ran her fingers over his loosened navy blue tie. "Your room or mine?"

This was it. This was the situation he'd been trying to avoid since he'd laid eyes on Mackenzie Carter. The old Alex wouldn't have hesitated to drag Mac to his hotel room and explore her delicious body. However, the new and improved Alex didn't think it was such a good idea. His right and wrong consciousness battled with one another, each arguing their point of view, trying to convince him to take their side. *This should be an easy decision. Say no, remain celibate, and send Mac on her merry way.*

"What will it be, Mr. Carter?" She brought her plump lips to his ear. "Do you want to share a night of unrestrained bliss with yours truly?" She tugged his earlobe between her teeth before soothing the bite with a kiss.

What. The. Fuck. If there was a book on seduction, Mac must have invented it. When she boldly ran her hips over his mid-section, he lost all train of thought. His eyes landed on hers and held her gaze.

"Mine," he said in a firm voice. "It's time that I show you what calling me 'Mr. Carter' does to me."

He didn't even give her a chance to respond as he tugged her through the garden and in the direction of Rosewood Inn.

ABOUT THE AUTHOR

Sherelle Green is a Chicago native with a dynamic imagination and a passion for reading and writing. Ever since she was a little girl, Sherelle has enjoyed story-telling. Upon receiving her BA in English, she decided to test her skills by composing a fifty-page romance. The short, but sweet, story only teased her creative mind, but it gave her the motivation she needed to follow her dream of becoming a published author.

Sherelle loves connecting with readers and other literary enthusiasts, and she is a member of RWA and NINC. She's also an Emma award winner and two-time RT Book Reviews nominee. Sherelle enjoys composing novels that are emotionally driven and convey real relationships and real-life issues that touch on subjects that may pull at your heart-strings. Nothing satisfies her more than writing stories filled with compelling love affairs, multifaceted characters, and intriguing relationships.

For more information:
www.sherellegreen.com
authorsherellegreen.com

ALSO BY SHERELLE GREEN

An Elite Event Series:
A Tempting Proposal
If Only for Tonight
Red Velvet Kisses
Beautiful Surrender

Bare Sophistication Series:
Enticing Winter
Falling for Autumn
Waiting for Summer
Nights of Fantasy
Her Unexpected Valentine

Additional Books:
A Miami Affair
Wrapped in Red

Made in the USA
Columbia, SC
15 May 2022